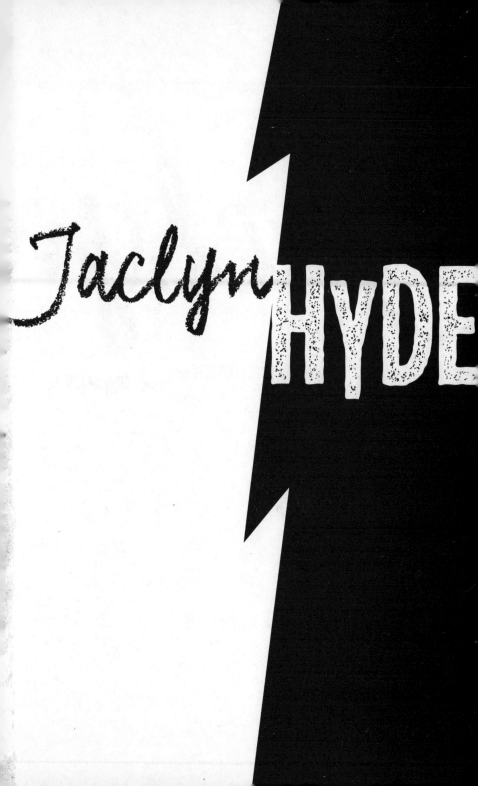

Jaclyn

by ANNABETH BONDOR-STONE *and* CONNOR WHITE

HYDE

HARPER

An Imprint of HarperCollinsPublishers

HYDE

For Ana, Ella, and Noah

Jaclyn Hyde

Copyright © 2019 by Annabeth Bondor-Stone and Connor White

Library of Congress Cataloging-in-Publication Data

Names: Bondor-Stone, Annabeth, author. | White, Connor, author.
Title: Jaclyn Hyde / by Annabeth Bondor-Stone and Connor White.
Description: New York, NY : HarperCollins, 2019. | Summary: "In this modern retelling of The
   Strange Case of Dr. Jekyll and Mr. Hyde, a girl's quest to be perfect unleashes chaos at her middle
   school"-- Provided by publisher.
Identifiers: LCCN 2018055866 | ISBN 978-0-06-267145-5 (hardback)
Subjects: | CYAC: Perfectionism (Personality trait)--Fiction. | Behavior--Fiction. |
   Supernatural--Fiction. | Middle schools--Fiction. | Schools--Fiction. | BISAC: JUVENILE
   FICTION / Fantasy & Magic. | JUVENILE FICTION / Mysteries & Detective Stories. |
   JUVENILE FICTION / Action & Adventure / General.
Classification: LCC PZ7.1.B665 Jac 2019 | DDC [Fic]--dc23 LC record available at
   https://lccn.loc.gov/2018055866

Typography by Joe Merkel
19 20 21 22 23   CG/LSCH   10 9 8 7 6 5 4 3 2 1
❖✳
First Edition

PROLOGUE

Dr. Enfield placed his lab mice inside the maze and started the timer. The three mice took off. In last place, as usual, was Mouse #1, who Dr. Enfield affectionately called Peanut. She always seemed to lag behind the others. After a minute had passed, Mouse #2 and Mouse #3 were halfway to the finish line. Peanut had gotten confused and was now trapped in a dead end.

That's when it happened.

Her tiny mouse nails grew into thick yellow claws. Her soft gray fur became wiry and matted. Her teeth sharpened into fangs. And Peanut realized that there was a faster way to the finish line.

She took a big bite out of the wall in front of her and plowed through headfirst. When she reached the next wall, she tore through it with her claws. Knocking down wall after wall, she headed straight for the piece of cheese at the end of the maze.

She was almost there when she saw Mouse #2. She let out an angry screech. It was a sound no normal mouse had ever made. Peanut bit down on Mouse #2's tail, then climbed over his head to reach the finish line first. She gobbled up the cheese in one bite.

But Peanut wasn't finished. She chomped through the thick outer wall of the maze and leaped out onto the lab table. She scurried toward an open window, knocking into a glass beaker, sending it crashing to the ground. She climbed onto the windowsill. Then she looked back at Dr. Enfield. Her eyes glowed bright green.

Dr. Enfield dropped his notebook. "What have I done?" he whispered as Peanut jumped out of the window and disappeared into the foggy night.

CHAPTER ONE
Fog Island: The Musical

Mr. Collins clapped his hands. "Five minutes until showtime," he announced.

The cast and crew of the eighth grade musical gathered backstage. This was the final dress rehearsal before the opening night of *Fog Island: The Musical*, an original musical based on the history of their town.

Mr. Collins paced between the empty auditorium seats. "You should all have your costumes on and your props in place. And I want to see a wig on every head."

Jaclyn Hyde pulled a loose thread from her costume, a red checkered pioneer dress. She straightened the dress and checked that her boots were evenly tied. Then she ran her hands over her pigtails to make sure there wasn't a single hair out of place. She was ready. She had practiced the dance steps in front of the mirror for weeks. She knew every last toe tap. She had run through the songs every night at her piano until she could sing them in her sleep— and sometimes, according to her parents, she *did* sing them in her sleep.

As Jaclyn took her spot in the dimly lit wings just offstage, she thought about what a shame it was that no one would see her perform. She was the understudy. But still, she was determined to be the most perfect understudy the world would never see.

Jaclyn strove for perfection in everything she did. She got nothing less than straight As. She packed as many activities into her schedule as possible and tried to do each one better than the last. There was a poster in the school guidance counselor's office that said, "Shoot for the moon. Even if you miss, you'll end up among the stars." Jaclyn never liked that poster. She thought that if you did the math correctly, you shouldn't miss the moon in the first place.

Jaclyn peered out at all the other students starting to take their places onstage and sighed. She decided to use the next few minutes to practice the opening dance one more time.

"One, two, kick, turn!" she whispered to herself as she sped through the steps. She finished the number, bending down on one knee and throwing her hands high in the air. She paused for a moment to catch her breath.

Then she heard clapping. Standing behind her was Fatima Ali, leaning coolly against the brick wall of the auditorium, her straight black hair pushed back by the sunglasses on her head.

"You must be the hardest working understudy in the history of theater," said Fatima.

Jaclyn smiled bashfully. "I don't know about that."

"Well, at least the history of *this* theater." Fatima gestured toward the Fog Island Middle School auditorium, with its peeling green velvet seats and beige carpet. She took a step forward and stumbled over a warped floorboard. "This place could really use an upgrade. Nothing has changed since it was built in October 1992."

Fatima was the editor of the school newspaper and knew almost everything there was to know about their school. She also knew almost everything there was to know about Fog Island. That's why Mr. Collins had asked her to help him write *Fog Island: The Musical.*

"Fatima, I need to speak with you before we start the show," Mr. Collins shouted from the front row.

"Be right there!" Fatima rolled her eyes. "It's probably about that stupid moose costume again . . ."

Several years before, Mr. Collins had purchased a very realistic (and very expensive) moose costume, and he was obsessed with finding a way to incorporate it into every musical. Last year, he directed *The Three Moose-keteers*, and the year before that *The Sound of Moose-ic* and before that, *Foot Moose*. He loved that costume and was extremely disappointed when Fatima informed him that there were no moose on Fog Island, and so he would have to hang up the costume until next year's production, which he had already decided would either be *The Moose-ic Man*, or an original adaptation of *Cats* called *Moose*.

Paige Greer ran over to Jaclyn and Fatima. She was covered in cardboard branches and paper leaves. Her face was painted green, and there were twigs sticking out of her hair.

"What's my line again?" she asked.

"'It sure is foggy out!'" Fatima reminded her.

"Right!" said Paige.

Paige had only agreed to be in the musical because Fatima and Jaclyn were doing it. The three of them spent as much time together as possible. Plus, the show happened to fall during the off-season between soccer and basketball. Paige didn't even think twice about diving face-first into the dirt when she was protecting the goal, but she was terrified of public speaking. That's why Fatima had written a special part for her: the Tree. It was perfect because Paige was the tallest kid in school, and she had only one line. Still, she was nervous about remembering it.

It sure is foggy out, Paige mouthed to herself. "I think I got it."

Shane Zeigler stomped backstage, carrying a heavy box. Shane always had a grin on his face like he knew something everybody else didn't. He stopped behind Jaclyn. "Move it, loser, VIP coming through! Very Important Props!"

"Okay, okay," Jaclyn said, stepping aside.

He sidled up to her. "By the way, Mr. Collins wanted me to give you something."

"What is it?" Jaclyn said, reaching out her hand.

"This!" Shane took a glob of glistening blue gum out of his mouth and planted it smack in the middle of her palm.

"Ugh! Gross!" Jaclyn flung the gum off her hand onto the floor.

Shane snorted with laughter.

"Beat it, vermin," Fatima snapped.

"Yeah!" said Paige. Then she turned to Fatima and whispered, "Wait, what's a vermin?"

Shane ignored them and pointed at his gum. "Hey, Jaclyn, if you're hungry, there might still be some broccoli in there from lunch!" He cackled, and Jaclyn could see bright-blue gum juice coating his braces.

Mr. Collins popped behind the curtain and scowled. "Shane, stop goofing off! I told you ten minutes ago to set up the props and plug in the fog machine. It's not that difficult."

Shane hadn't signed up to be a stagehand. He'd been caught trying to flush a pie down the toilet in the teacher's lounge, and had been forced to help out with the musical as a punishment. Before Shane could respond, Mr. Collins spotted the gum on the floor. "Is that your gum? Clean that up this instant! Why can't you be more like Jaclyn Hyde? She never causes any problems. Honestly, you would do well to take a page out of her book."

Shane gave Jaclyn a withering stare. "Little Miss Perfect," he said, shaking his head. He picked up his gum and skulked away.

Mr. Collins spotted Fatima. "Fatima! There you are. What would you say to a moose dream sequence?"

"*No!*" Fatima insisted.

Mr. Collins sighed. "Well, it was worth a try." He hurried away and took his seat at the piano.

Jaclyn turned to Paige and Fatima. "Why is Shane always so mean to me?"

"Because he's a lizard spawn," said Fatima.

Jaclyn frowned. "He's been this way ever since third grade, when he broke my flamingo."

When Jaclyn was in third grade, her class

went on a field trip to an art studio. They each got to paint their own piece of pottery. All the other kids chose something simple—a mug, a bowl, a plate—but Jaclyn chose an elaborate flamingo figurine. She painstakingly painted each individual feather a different shade of pink and was almost finished when Shane snuck up and smashed the head right off it. Jaclyn had no idea why he'd done it then, or for that matter, why he continued to torment her now.

Fatima shrugged. "Everyone has a Shane. That one person who won't stop bugging you."

"That's true," said Paige. "Remember Winston? He repeated everything I said."

Fatima arched her eyebrow. "Paige, Winston was your parrot."

"Yeah. And he was really annoying."

Mr. Collins's voice rang through the auditorium. "Places, everybody! Let's take it from the top."

Paige took her place at the back of the stage. Fatima went out into the audience to watch.

Jaclyn stood in the wings as the curtain rose, and Mr. Collins banged out the notes of the first musical number, "This Land Is Fog Land." It was an elaborate song about how the early settlers stumbled upon the island completely by accident when their boat crashed in the fog. Singing front and center was Marina Littlefield. Marina was playing the lead role of Penny Pogwilly, founder of Fog Island and the narrator of the musical. Jaclyn couldn't help but feel a twinge of jealousy being Marina's understudy. No matter how well Jaclyn knew the part, there was no denying Marina's naturally beautiful singing voice, which landed her the lead role in the musical every year.

Jaclyn mirrored Marina's every move off-stage, mouthing the words to the song as Marina belted them out loud. Jaclyn hit every beat perfectly, even the complicated shuffle step that caused Marina to trip over her own feet. They reached the end of the number, and everyone landed in the exact right position at the exact right moment. It was the first time that had ever happened.

Mr. Collins was thrilled. "Fantastic work, everyone." He was about to begin the second song when they heard booing from the back row.

The principal, Miss Carver, marched up the aisle. She had a hunched back and a face so sharp-featured she looked like a vulture. Her gray hair was plaited in a tight braid that went down to her waist. She wore a stiff woolen skirt and sweater that made the students itch just by looking at it. "THAT WAS DISGRACEFUL!" she barked.

Mr. Collins jumped up from the piano. "Miss Carver! I didn't know you were here."

"I wish I *wasn't*. I'll never be able to unsee what I just saw!" She banged her fist on the stage, where the students were frozen in fear. "You were spinning when you should have been twirling! *You* were twirling when you should have been tapping! And *you* were tapping when you should have been leaving the stage altogether!"

Jaclyn took a step onstage. "Miss Carver," she said sweetly, "if you don't mind my saying, the whole cast has been working really hard—"

"I DO MIND YOU SAYING!" Miss Carver snapped. She jabbed her finger at Jaclyn. "You were the worst of all!"

Jaclyn's lip quivered. "How? I wasn't even onstage."

"Then why could I *see* you? The understudy is supposed to be completely out of sight, not hovering in the wings hoping for a moment in the spotlight!"

Jaclyn's heart sank.

Miss Carver stomped over to Mr. Collins, who backed up until he was against the brick wall. "You'd better get your act together before opening night," she sneered. "If you embarrass me, I'll tear down this auditorium and turn it into the school dumpster!"

Fatima piped up, "Actually, until 1998, it was both the auditorium *and* the school dumpster."

Miss Carver turned to her. "Silence, you

know-it-all!" She glared at the cast. "Ironic, isn't it? That a musical about the history of Fog Island will go down as the worst musical in the history of Fog Island!" She turned on her heel and stormed out.

Mr. Collins let out a long, slow exhale. "Everybody take five."

Fatima went backstage and found Jaclyn sitting with her head in her hands.

"I can't believe I messed up like that," said Jaclyn. "I didn't realize anyone could see me."

Fatima put her hand on Jaclyn's shoulder. "Give yourself a break. Miss Carver is crazy. Besides, you're already painting the set, designing the programs, and bringing snacks for the whole cast every day. You don't have to be perfect at everything."

Yes I do, thought Jaclyn. But she didn't say it out loud.

CHAPTER TWO
Who's Ready to Science?

Jaclyn poured exactly one hundred sixty-four chocolate chips into the cookie batter. She was home from rehearsal, standing at the kitchen counter making a batch of Grandma Hyde's Chocolate Delights. Her family's cookie recipe had been passed down for generations. All the ingredients were perfectly proportioned to make the world's best chocolate chip cookie. Jaclyn dug in the wooden spoon and stirred exactly twenty-three times, just as the recipe instructed.

"Whose birthday is it tomorrow?" her dad asked, peering into the bowl of batter.

"Darcy Lithgow," Jaclyn replied.

Jaclyn always baked treats for her classmates' birthdays. She had a calendar in her room with every birthday written in red so she wouldn't forget anyone.

"That's my perfect little girl," said Dad. He took a sip from a mug that said *World's Luckiest Dad*. Jaclyn's father owned a screen-printing business. He designed Fog Island T-shirts, mugs, and bumper stickers that were sold in souvenir shops all over town. In his spare time, he designed items for himself that were often decorated with some embarrassing sentiment about how much he loved his daughters.

Jaclyn's mom came downstairs. "Oh! Grandma Hyde's Chocolate Delights! Must be somebody's birthday tomorrow." She pulled a small spoon out of the silverware drawer and tasted the batter. "Jaclyn, did you remember the half teaspoon of cinnamon?"

"Yes, Mom," Jaclyn said, spooning small scoops of batter onto the cookie sheet.

Mom smiled and kissed her on the forehead. "Of course you did." She wiped some flour off the counter with a damp towel. "Remember, clean as you go."

"I know, Mom, I'm just trying to get the cookies in before Paige and Fatima get here to work on our science fair project."

"Let me help," said Mom. She spooned out the rest of the batter, and then put the cookie tray in the oven. She checked her watch. "When did it get so late? We have to get to the post office."

"Just putting the final touches on the package," Dad said, slapping a big red bow onto a box wrapped in brown paper. "Melanie is going to love this." Jaclyn's sister, Melanie, was away at college. Her parents sent her a care package every time she got an A on a test—which meant that they were at the post office practically every week. Melanie had always gotten perfect grades, excelled at every after-school activity, and even once won the Fog Island Community Service Award for delivering meals to the elderly. It was all Jaclyn could do to try to keep up.

Mom grabbed her coat. "Jaclyn, are you going to be okay with the oven on?"

Dad winked at her. "She can handle the responsibility. She's Jaclyn Hyde."

"Yeah, Mom. How many times have we made chocolate delights together? I know the drill."

"Okay, then. Just remember to clean Charles's cage today."

"I will, Mom." Jaclyn forced a smile. "I clean it every week—just like I promised."

"And you've got that history test tomorrow. You're going to study?"

"I'll study after I finish working on the science fair project," she said, ushering her parents toward the front door. "It'll all get done! It always does."

"I'm only asking because I care," said Mom.

"We'll be back soon," said Dad. "We love you!"

Jaclyn's parents walked out and closed the door behind them.

"And one last thing . . . ," Jaclyn said to herself, knowing what was coming next.

The door swung open again and Jaclyn's mom popped her head in. "And one last thing: When you take the cookies out, don't forget to use an oven mitt."

"I *won't!*" Jaclyn said, exasperated.

After her parents finally left, Jaclyn hung up her apron. She looked at the clock. It was 3:57. She had three minutes until her friends were supposed to arrive. She decided she would get started on cleaning the rabbit cage. She went upstairs to her bedroom. Charles's cage was placed neatly on top of her dresser so that Charles could look out the window. He liked looking out the window. He also liked munching on the wood chips that lined the floor of his cage, which Jaclyn didn't understand, but she couldn't very well ask him to stop.

For months, Jaclyn had begged her parents to let her get a rabbit. Finally, she wrote up a three-page contract detailing how she would take care of her new pet—feeding him twice a day, keeping his water bottle full, and cleaning his cage every week. In the end, her parents agreed.

Jaclyn lifted up the cage. "Oof, Charles, you get heavier every week. Better lay off the wood chips for a while."

Charles looked up at her and wiggled his nose.

"You're right. You're adorable just the way you are!" She carried his cage down the stairs and put it on the kitchen counter. She dumped the old water down the drain. Then she put the dish towel over her arm like she was a server at a fancy restaurant.

"May I offer you some fresh water, sir?" she said.

Charles wiggled his nose.

"Coming right up." She filled up the water bottle and screwed it back into the side of the cage. "Room temperature, just how you like it. Today's special is weird brown rabbit food—"

Just then, the doorbell rang. Jaclyn opened it and saw Paige and Fatima on the doorstep.

Fatima eyed the dish towel draped on Jaclyn's arm. "Were you pretending to run a fancy restaurant for your rabbit again?"

"No!" Jaclyn whipped the towel off and stuffed it in her back pocket.

"So what if she was?" said Paige. "Doesn't Charles deserve the best?"

"My thoughts exactly," said Jaclyn.

Paige took off her neon-yellow windbreaker and tossed it across the hall, where it landed perfectly on the coat rack. "Who's ready to science?"

"I'm not sure you can use science as a verb," Fatima quipped.

Jaclyn looked at the clock again. "It's 4:02. You're late."

"Don't blame me," said Fatima. "We were riding our bikes over and Paige saw a group of ninth graders playing pickup basketball in the park. She wanted to see if she could score on them."

"Did you?" Jaclyn asked Paige.

"Twice!"

"Come on," Jaclyn said. "I've got everything set up in the garage." She hoisted Charles's cage and led the girls to the garage. Inside was a giant model of a volcano that reached halfway to the ceiling. Jaclyn wasn't going to settle for a project that would just go straight into the trash after getting a participation award. She wasn't going to show up with a plant growing under a black-light or a tooth decaying in a soda bottle. She was going to go above and beyond. Which is why she'd decided to build an exact replica of Mount Vesuvius, the deadly Italian volcano that erupted in the year 79 CE and destroyed the city of Pompeii.

"Whoa!" Paige shouted. Her jaw dropped.

She looked like the Pompeians had just before they met their demise.

Fatima shook her head. "Jaclyn, I thought we were supposed to make this together."

"We are! But I did a little extra work yesterday after I finished my homework before my piano lesson—"

"A *little* extra?" Fatima said, arching her eyebrow.

"Okay, fine. I papier-mâchéed the entire volcano, constructed the tiny town out of toothpicks, and double-checked the calculations to make sure it's all to scale. But we still have to paint all the people running away from the lava."

"Cool!" said Paige. She grabbed a paintbrush and smiled. "I bet I could outrun lava."

Fatima and Paige got to work painting the small figurines at the base of the volcano, while Jaclyn set up her home chemistry set to make the lava. She had created the recipe herself in order to concoct an eruption that would mimic the exact magnitude of Mount Vesuvius. She used the dropper to measure out a precise formula of vinegar, dish soap, and food dye. Then she added a few of her own special ingredients.

She held up the beaker of red liquid. "All set. Now, all we need to do is combine it with the baking soda and—kaboom! How's the town coming?"

"I still have to paint ten more faces," said Fatima, as she painted a screaming mouth onto one of the figurines.

"I'm just painting cool hats on all my people," said Paige.

Jaclyn figured she could use this extra time to clean out Charles's cage. She opened it up and started scooping all the old, soggy wood chips into a garbage bag.

"These people are so tiny," Fatima exclaimed in frustration.

"They're exactly to scale," said Jaclyn.

"Why are we putting all this work into a science fair that no one is even going to win?"

Paige stopped what she was doing. "What do you mean no one is going to win?"

"There hasn't been a winner for the past five years. Not since Miss Carver became principal," said Fatima. "Nothing is ever good enough for her."

"Which is exactly why we have to submit the greatest science project of all time," Jaclyn said, wiping down the floor of Charles's cage with a paper towel.

Fatima let out a huff. "No matter how amazing this project turns out, there's no way we're going to win the science fair. No one will."

"Maybe they should call it the science *un*fair," said Paige.

Fatima laughed. "Everything about that Miss Carver is unfair. She's the meanest principal ever! And you know I'm not exaggerating. Journalists never exaggerate."

Unfortunately for all the students at Fog Island Middle School, Fatima wasn't exaggerating.

She continued, "One time, she saw me

accidentally throw a plastic bottle in the trash can instead of the recycling bin. She made me climb in after it—and then she closed the lid on me!"

Paige nodded. "One time we were losing a basketball game. Coach was yelling at us. Then Miss Carver came over and started yelling at Coach. It was the first time I'd ever seen a grown-up cry. Plus, she wouldn't let me join the football team. She wouldn't even let me try out. She just assumed I wouldn't be good enough to play on the boys' team and that I would embarrass the school."

"I wish Mrs. Goodman was still the principal. I hear she was awesome," said Fatima.

"My sister talked about her all the time," said Jaclyn.

Before Miss Carver took over, the principal of Fog Island Middle School had been Greta Goodman. This was during the time that Melanie went to the school, and she always said how kind and encouraging Mrs. Goodman was.

Mrs. Goodman believed that all children had the potential to be great if they were treated with respect.

Jaclyn put down her cleaning supplies and found Melanie's old yearbook stacked on a dusty shelf in the back of the garage. She flipped through the pages until she found a picture of Mrs. Goodman handing Melanie a blue ribbon. "Look."

Fatima and Paige gathered around her. Fatima pointed at Mrs. Goodman, who had rosy cheeks, curly red hair, and a smiling face. "She looks like the opposite of Miss Carver."

"What's the blue ribbon for?" asked Paige.

"The science fair," said Jaclyn. "Melanie was the last person to win it."

"Well, yeah, because Mrs. Goodman was the judge," said Fatima. "Now that Miss Carver is the judge, nothing will ever be good enough."

"Plus, she smells like vinegar," said Paige.

"Excellent point," said Fatima.

"The science fair is next week. We just have

to stay on her good side until then," said Jaclyn.

"She doesn't have any good sides!" said Fatima. "They're all bad sides!"

"Well, we at least have to try." Jaclyn slammed the yearbook shut. "Is the town finished?"

"I'm done," said Fatima.

"I'm just putting a basketball in this guy's hand," said Paige.

"Hmm, that's not historically accurate. But I'll let it slide." Jaclyn climbed up onto a stepstool, carrying the lava mixture and a tablespoon of baking soda. "Ready to commence test eruption."

"Wait—you're going to set it off now?" said Paige. "We just spent all that time painting the people."

"Not to worry. The lava is water soluble. One quick spray-down and it'll be good as new. Now, stand back." She poured the baking soda into the volcano, and then added in the lava. She hopped down from the stepstool.

"Five . . . four . . . three . . . two—"

Before she could get to "one," a frothy red mixture bubbled up from the volcano and cascaded down the sides without any sign of stopping. In fact, the eruption just seemed to be getting bigger. There was a gurgling sound, and the volcano belched up a blob of lava that soared out of the garage and landed in the driveway.

"Whoa," said Jaclyn. "That's not supposed to happen."

Just then, she heard a muffled beeping sound.

"What is that?" she said.

"It's coming from the kitchen," said Fatima.

Paige cocked her head. "That's funny, I heard that same sound when my little brother melted all his action figures over the stove." She turned to Jaclyn. "Are *you* melting all your action figures over the stove?"

Then it dawned on Jaclyn what she was hearing. The fire alarm. She gasped. "Grandma Hyde's Chocolate Delights!"

Jaclyn sprinted into the house. The kitchen was filled with smoke. Jaclyn put on an oven mitt, flung open the oven door, pulled out the cookie sheet, and threw the whole smoking tray into the sink. Paige ran around like a chicken with its head cut off, flapping a dish towel to clear the air.

Ever the journalist, Fatima pulled out her phone and took a picture. "Wow, you two look just like all the figurines we just painted."

Jaclyn turned on the cold water, drenching the charred cookies. "They're ruined."

Paige patted her on the shoulder. "It's okay, Jaclyn. You've got all that lava in the garage. Why not make a lava cake?"

"That's not what a lava cake is, Paige," said Fatima.

"I can't believe I burned the cookies," Jaclyn wailed. "What am I going to do about Darcy's birthday?"

"Just go to the store and buy more cookie

dough," said Fatima.

Jaclyn looked at her like she was speaking a different language. "Are you crazy? I've made Chocolate Delights from scratch for every person's birthday since first grade. I can't switch to store-bought now. This is a disaster."

"No, *this* is a disaster," said Paige, standing at the door to the garage.

"What do you mean?" Jaclyn ran over to her. Mount Vesuvius had erupted everywhere. The whole garage was overflowing with foamy red suds that oozed out into the driveway.

"It looks like someone got murdered with bubble bath in here," said Paige.

"I must have made the lava formula too strong," said Jaclyn.

"That's the understatement of the century," said Fatima.

Jaclyn sloshed across the soaking-wet floor. The lava had splattered everywhere. It had coated Dad's power tools and soaked the stacks of books and papers on the shelves. It was even on the ceiling.

"How am I going to clean this up?" Jaclyn put her head in her hands. "This day could not get any worse."

Then she saw something that made her forget all about the volcano wreckage *and* the smoldering cookies in the sink. In the chaos, she had left the door of Charles's cage open. And now, Charles was gone.

CHAPTER THREE
Stay Away from Cedar Street

"*Charles?! Charles?!*" Jaclyn shouted.

She, Paige, and Fatima ran frantically around the front yard looking for the rabbit. A thick fog hung in the air, and a biting wind whipped up the dried leaves that lay scattered across the ground. The girls searched in the bushes and under the front porch. Paige even looked under the doormat.

Jaclyn tugged at her hair. "How could I leave

the cage open? You never leave the cage open. That's the number one rule of owning a rabbit!"

"Don't worry. We'll find him," Paige said. "Let me get a better view." She climbed up the birch tree in the middle of the yard.

"Any sign of him?" said Fatima.

Paige scanned the area. "No . . . But there are a couple of squirrels up here. Do you want a pet squirrel, Jaclyn?"

"No! I want Charles!" Jaclyn wailed.

Jaclyn hadn't been this frazzled since last spring, when she forgot to wear green to school on Saint Patrick's Day. Fatima grabbed Jaclyn by the shoulders. "Breathe, Jaclyn. Breathe."

"I don't have time to breathe!" Jaclyn protested. "If my parents come home and find out that I lost Charles, they'll disown me."

"No, they won't."

"Well then, I'll disown myself!"

"Jaclyn, you're overreacting."

"No, you're underreacting!"

"Hey, look!" By now, Paige had climbed

down from the tree and was pointing across the street. "Is that one of Charles's wood chips?"

Sure enough, on the pavement next to the storm drain was a thin shaving of yellow wood. Jaclyn's eyes grew wide. They all darted across the street, then crouched down and peered into the storm drain.

"Charles! Are you down there?" Jaclyn shouted, her voice echoing off the sewer walls. "Why did I get such a quiet pet?"

Fatima leaned closer to the storm drain and squinted into the darkness. "I can't see anything . . ." She pushed herself up. "Ugh! But I can smell *everything*."

"What if he's trapped down there? He can't swim!"

"How do you know? Maybe he can swim," said Paige.

Fatima sighed. "Paige, I love your optimism, but let's be honest. He probably can't swim."

Paige narrowed her eyes and stared down the street through the fog. "Is that him?"

All the way at the end of the block, Charles was hopping along the sidewalk. Had it not been for his brown spots, he would have vanished into the fog altogether.

Jaclyn's face lit up. "Nice job, Paige. You've got eagle eyes!"

"Don't you mean rabbit eyes?" said Paige, confused.

The girls ran after Charles as fast as they could, but he hopped down the street even faster. They passed a row of houses and had almost caught up to him when he suddenly turned and hopped in another direction. The wrong direction. The worst direction he could have turned.

Jaclyn gasped. "He went down Cedar Street!"

Jaclyn had never been down Cedar Street. None of them had. Cedar Street was a dead end, empty except for one house that every kid on Fog Island avoided at all costs—Enfield Manor. It was an abandoned estate where a mad scientist named Cornelius Enfield used to live. The warnings had been whispered down through generations of Fog Island kids, from older siblings to younger siblings, from middle schoolers to elementary schoolers, from babysitters to babysitees. The message was clear as could be: *Stay away from Cedar Street.*

Fatima put her hands on her hips. "It can't really be that bad. It's just a street with a big empty house at the end!"

"The *dead* end!" said Paige, biting her fingernails.

Jaclyn took a deep breath. "Fatima's right. It's just a dumb street. My parents will be home any minute. We have to find Charles."

"Then it's decided," said Fatima, nudging Jaclyn forward. "Let's go."

The girls turned the corner onto Cedar Street. Paige lagged a step behind. Even though she was the tallest, strongest, and definitely the fastest of the three of them, she was also the most easily spooked. She was very superstitious. Once she accidentally broke a mirror and spent three weeks gluing it back together. She even carried a rabbit's foot key chain for good luck, but she couldn't very well use it now—that just felt wrong.

"There he is," said Jaclyn, pointing just up ahead.

They ran down the street, which was lined on both sides with moss-covered trees and overgrown weeds. They found Charles sitting in front of Enfield Manor's wrought-iron gate. He was wiggling his nose, completely oblivious to the fact that he was planted in front of the scariest house on the island. Three stories high, with walls of dark-gray brick and a pitched roof of black shale, the house seemed like the kind of place that would attract a lightning bolt in a thunderstorm. The windows were shuttered and the shutters were locked, except for one on the ground floor that creaked back and forth in the wind. A stone path led from the gate to the front door. At the base of the front steps were two unlit gas lanterns.

Jaclyn held out her hands to stop Paige and

Fatima from getting any closer. "Be careful," she said softly. "We can't scare him. The last thing I want is for him to run through that gate."

The girls nodded in agreement.

Jaclyn got down on one knee and held out her hands like she was making an offering to a saint. "Come here, Charles," she said in her sweetest voice. "Come here, buddy."

Except for his nose, Charles didn't move.

Fatima decided to take a more logical approach. "Charles, think this through. What does this house have to offer that Jaclyn's doesn't? There are no wood chips. I bet there isn't even any running water. So let's end this silly game of chase, and you march your fuzzy little butt right back over here."

Charles didn't budge.

"Guys, don't be ridiculous. He can't understand you!" said Paige. "I got this." She pulled her wrists up to her shoulders and balled up her fists like little bunny paws. Then she wiggled her nose and started hopping up and down.

As the all-time leading rebounder on the Fog Island Middle School basketball team, Paige could really hop.

Jaclyn looked at Paige like she was crazy. "What are you doing?"

"I'm speaking to him in his language," Paige explained, hopping from side to side.

Fatima couldn't help herself and let out a giggle. Charles jumped backward.

"Everybody stop!" Jaclyn whispered. "Let me do this." She was on both knees now, her hands clasped together. "Charles, please, please come over here. I can't lose you. You're an indoor bunny. You can't survive out here. Come on, buddy . . . please?" When Charles still didn't move, Jaclyn couldn't take it anymore. Finally, she shouted, "Charles Benedict Hyde, come over here right now!"

Startled, Charles turned and ran between the bars of the gate.

"That worked well," Fatima said.

Jaclyn ran up to the iron gate and grabbed

the bars. Charles hopped along the stone path all the way to the front door. When the wind caught the shutter of the first-floor window, Charles looked at it curiously, and then hopped toward it.

"Oh, no . . . ," said Jaclyn.

Charles leaped onto the windowsill and scurried into the house.

"What are we going to do?" Jaclyn cried, whirling around to Paige and Fatima.

"There's only one thing we can do," said Fatima.

"No way! I'm not going in there!" said Paige, her eyes bulging. "A mad scientist lives there! There's probably a bunch of dead zombies inside!"

"Technically zombies are *un*dead," Fatima corrected her.

Jaclyn knew she shouldn't sneak into someone's house. On the other hand, nobody *lived* in this house. It was a dead guy's house. And she couldn't imagine a dead guy would mind too much. She could just run inside, scoop up Charles, and take him back home. Nobody would have to know that any of this ever happened.

She turned back to her friends just as Fatima was saying, "No, *werewolves* change under a full moon. Zombies eat brains!"

"I'm going in!" Jaclyn announced. "Who's with me?"

"I am," said Fatima. "I've always been curious about this house."

"Forget it! Not me!" Paige said.

"You'd rather stand outside by yourself?"

"Yes." Paige looked around the creepy street. "I mean no." Her shoulders slumped. "Okay, fine. I'll go."

Jaclyn lifted the latch on the gate. To her surprise, it swung open easily. The girls crept up to the house, Paige glancing nervously over her shoulder. Jaclyn tried the front door.

"It's locked." She sighed.

"Well, if the window is good enough for

Charles . . . ," said Fatima. She walked over to the open window and climbed inside. Jaclyn and Paige followed.

They found themselves in a sitting room. The furniture was covered in dusty white sheets.

Fatima wandered over to the corner, where there was a large wooden clock with a pendulum that had stopped swinging long ago. "This grandfather clock must be really old," she said.

Paige joined her. "Yeah. I bet it's actually a great-grandfather clock."

Jaclyn crouched down and looked under the couch. "Charles? Charles?" she whispered. It was hard to see in the dim light, but she could tell he wasn't there. She walked over to a closet under a wooden staircase. She cracked open the door. Inside was an overcoat, a raincoat, and a dingy white lab coat.

Fatima looked over Jaclyn's shoulder. "I could write a whole series of articles about this place!" She took out her phone and started snapping pictures.

"We have to find Charles and get out of here," said Jaclyn. She hurried into the next room, but what she saw inside stopped her dead in her tracks. "Whoa!" she called out. "You've got to see this."

Paige and Fatima followed her voice to a decrepit science lab. Cloudy glass beakers and test tubes full of murky liquid lined the shelves. There were old cracked microscopes and what looked like a dead jellyfish floating in a jar. There was a glass display case of insect bodies hanging on the wall.

Fatima approached a rusty metal desk in the middle of the room. "What do you think is in here?"

Before Jaclyn could respond, Paige yelled out, "Hey! I found Charles!"

Fatima and Jaclyn whipped around and saw Paige chasing after a furry creature with wiry gray fur, thick yellow claws, and bright green eyes.

"Paige! That's a rat!!" Jaclyn shouted.

Paige came to a halt. She thought for a second. Then smiled. "Hey! I found a rat!" She chased after it again.

"She never ceases to amaze me," said Fatima. She opened the desk drawer and pulled out a heavy, leather-bound notebook. Her eyes sparkled. "Jackpot!"

Jaclyn looked over Fatima's shoulder. She knew that she should focus on finding Charles, but she was just too curious. Fatima flipped through the pages, which were filled with handwritten scribblings.

"These look like records of all his experiments," said Fatima.

Something caught Jaclyn's eye. "Wait!" she said. She flipped back through the notebook until she found the page again. At the top was written, "Perfection Potion," followed by some kind of formula.

Jaclyn and Fatima locked eyes.

"What do you think it does?" Jaclyn whispered.

Fatima didn't respond.

Paige's voice cut through the silence. "Uh . . . guys?" she called from the sitting room. "Weren't the lanterns in the front yard *out* when we came in here?"

"What?" said Fatima, dashing over to her.

Without thinking, Jaclyn ripped out the page from the notebook and stuffed it in her pocket. She shoved the notebook back in the drawer, and then ran to join her friends. They all looked out the open window. The gas lanterns at the front steps were now lit.

Then they heard a key turn in the front door.

CHAPTER FOUR
Do Not Open

Click.

The front door of Enfield Manor unlocked. As the knob began to turn, Jaclyn's eyes darted to the coat closet beneath the staircase. She grabbed Paige and Fatima by their wrists and pulled them inside. She closed the closet door just as the front door opened. They huddled together, peering through the slats.

A man walked into the house. He was older

and tired-looking, with a scruffy gray beard and weathered skin. He wore brown overalls, heavy boots, and a white shirt stained with red splotches. His hands were large and calloused. He carried a gray canvas duffel bag over his shoulder. Whatever was inside the bag clanked as he walked.

Paige gripped Jaclyn's arm and whispered, "Is he a werewolf?" She turned to Fatima. "I thought you said werewolves only come out during a full moon!"

Jaclyn gritted her teeth. "Shh! You're going to get us caught."

Fatima pulled out her phone and started talking softly into it. "This is Fatima Ali. I'm here in the coat closet at Enfield Manor—"

What are you doing?! Jaclyn mouthed.

"Taking notes for an article. This is a journalist's dream. Nobody knows anything about Enfield Manor. If I can break this story, forget the school newspaper—I'll get hired by the *Fog Island Times*."

"The only thing that's going to be in the *Fog Island Times* is our mug shots. Put your phone down." Jaclyn grabbed for the phone. Fatima pulled her hand away. In the scuffle, the phone dropped to the ground with a thud.

The girls froze. Paige held her breath. Through the slats in the door, Jaclyn saw the man take a step toward the closet. Then another. The wooden floorboards creaked beneath his boots. He reached out and grabbed the doorknob. Jaclyn's stomach twisted into a knot.

Then, she heard a scratching sound above her. Something was scurrying around on the second floor. The man looked up.

"Darn rats," he said, his voice low and hoarse. He turned and walked up the stairs. The girls heard his heavy boots stomping above them.

"Now's our chance!" Jaclyn whispered.

They sprinted out of the closet, and out the front door. They tore across the yard, kicking up the gravel as they ran. None of them dared to look back to see if the man had caught a glimpse of them. They kept on running until they turned the corner off Cedar Street.

When they were safely out of sight, Fatima stopped and bent over, clutching her side to catch her breath. "Can we please stop running now?

"That was terrifying!" said Jaclyn.

"I hated every second of it!" said Paige. "Except for the part with the rat. That was pretty cool. But the rest was awful!"

"Who was that guy?" Fatima wondered aloud. "And what do you think was in that bag? An ax? A chainsaw?"

A look of fear crossed Paige's face. "A smaller bag?!"

Jaclyn didn't say anything. She slumped down on the curb and put her head in her hands. Fatima and Paige sat down next to her. Without even asking, they both knew what was on her mind.

Fatima put her arm around Jaclyn. "It's okay. I'm sure Charles will make his way home."

Paige added, "He has an excellent sense of direction. He'll miss you too much and then he'll hop on back."

Jaclyn's forehead creased with worry. "I hope you're right."

When Jaclyn, Paige, and Fatima got back to Jaclyn's house, her mom was standing in the front yard, tapping her foot impatiently, her arms crossed.

"Jaclyn Isabelle Hyde," her mom called out.

Jaclyn winced. She hated her middle name. But that was because she only ever heard it when she was in trouble.

"Oh no . . . ," said Jaclyn. "The garage." She had totally forgotten about the mess. The door was still open, and everything inside was coated in frothy red lava.

Fatima turned to Jaclyn. "Remember when you said this day couldn't get any worse?"

Jaclyn's mom met them at the sidewalk. "Young lady . . ."

"I know, Mom. You're disappointed—" said Jaclyn.

"Disappointed doesn't even begin to describe it. How in the world did Mount Vesuvius erupt all over the tools, the Ping-Pong table, and the lawn mower?"

"I'm sorry. I'm still tinkering with the lava formula. I was going to clean it up—"

Her mom interrupted, "And you burned the cookies. We trusted you, Jaclyn. You could have burned the whole house down. What in the world was so important that you'd leave the house in such a state anyway?"

Fatima and Paige looked at Jaclyn.

"Uh . . . well . . . ," Jaclyn began. She had no idea what to say. But she knew she couldn't bring herself to tell her mom that she'd lost Charles. "We went to buy more cookie dough . . ."

Jaclyn's mom looked surprised. "Store-bought cookie dough?"

"I know, Mom, but I—"

"So, where is it?" Mom interrupted.

"Where's what?" Jaclyn asked.

"The cookie dough."

"Oh . . . ," said Jaclyn. "Um . . ."

Fatima piped up, "Paige ate it!"

"I did?" said Paige. "I did. I was *really* hungry."

Jaclyn's mom gave Paige a concerned look. Then she turned back to Jaclyn. "Well, I don't even know where to begin. Your father is very upset. He loves that lawn mower."

Jaclyn looked down.

"Did you at least remember to clean Charles's cage?" said Mom.

Jaclyn swallowed hard. "Of course I did."

After Paige and Fatima went home, Jaclyn flipped through her science notebook and found the lava formula. She couldn't figure out what had gone wrong. It was supposed to flow down the model of Mount Vesuvius, not explode everywhere. The formula was a failure. She ripped the page out of the notebook and folded it up. She went to the storage shed in the back-yard. It was overgrown with weeds. Her parents barely ever went inside. She scooted toward the back corner, where she'd hidden a cardboard box that said DO NOT OPEN. She lifted the lid and put the formula inside, on top of an old math test that she'd gotten a C+ on and didn't want her parents to find. She closed the box and put it back in its hiding place.

Later, Jaclyn mopped the floor of the garage. She couldn't believe she'd ruined the cookies, totally trashed the garage, lost Charles (possibly forever), snuck into someone else's house, nearly been killed by some sort of werewolf man, and *lied* about all of it.

Jaclyn squeezed out the mop, dripping the last of the bright red lava into the soapy bucket. Then she used a damp sponge to clean her dad's tools, the Ping-Pong table, and the volcano. It took a while, but when she was done, every-thing looked as good as new. Then she spotted Charles's cage still sitting in the corner of the garage. Her mom must not have noticed it in the mess. Jaclyn took off her shoes, then folded up her white socks into a ball that kind of looked like Charles, at least from far away. She put the sock ball in the cage and carried the whole setup back up to her room. She passed by her parents, who were reading in the living room.

"All clean, Jaclyn?" her mom asked.

"It's like Mount Vesuvius never erupted," said Jaclyn. She turned to her dad. "I'm really sorry."

Dad didn't look up from his book. "Me too. I thought you could handle the responsibility."

Jaclyn stared down at the floor. "Mom?" she said softly. "Can you drive the volcano to school on Friday on your way to work? Our science teacher wants to see how all the projects are going before the fair next week."

Mom gave her a concerned look. "Will it be ready in time?"

Jaclyn nodded. "The volcano is fine. I just need to rethink the lava formula."

Jaclyn put Charles's cage on the dresser, and then collapsed on her bed. She stared up at the ceiling. What had happened to her? She was Jaclyn Hyde! She was supposed to be perfect! And this was about as far from perfect as she could ever imagine. That's when she remembered the crumpled piece of paper from Dr. Enfield's lab. She pulled it out of her pocket and laid it on the bedspread.

"Perfection Potion," she whispered to herself.

CHAPTER FIVE
Rotten Apples Fresh from the Tree

Jaclyn read through all the ingredients of the Perfection Potion. She realized she had almost everything she needed in her chemistry set. There was just one ingredient on the list that she didn't have.

Rotten apples fresh from the tree.

What could that mean? she thought. It was hard to imagine how an apple could be rotten and fresh at the same time. She had never seen or heard of anything like that before. But if she needed to find a special kind of apple, there was only one place to start: the Fog Island Orchard.

Fog Island was famous for its apples, known far and wide as the best in the world. The orchard was the pride of the island. And it was just a quick bike ride away. Now all she needed was an excuse to leave the house. Could she go to Paige's for dinner? *No,* she thought, *I'm in too much trouble for that.* Maybe she could return an overdue library book. The only problem was, she hadn't had an overdue library book since—well, ever. She looked out the window. The afternoon light was starting to fade. Whatever she was going to do, she had to do it fast.

That's when she heard her mom's voice downstairs. "David, we're out of milk. Will you go to the store?"

"Yes, dear!" he called back.

This was her chance. Jaclyn flew down the

stairs. Just before she got to the kitchen she slowed down her pace—she didn't want to seem *too* eager.

"I'll go!" Jaclyn said.

Her mom eyed her skeptically. "Don't you have homework to do?"

"It's done," said Jaclyn.

Jaclyn's parents looked at each other like they were communicating telepathically.

"Okay, then," said Mom.

Jaclyn almost blurted out, *Thank you*, but then she caught herself. What kid thanks their parents for letting them run errands?

"Go straight there and back. And wear your reflective helmet—it's foggy out," said Dad. "What am I saying? It's always foggy out."

Jaclyn hopped on her bike and pedaled as fast as she could in the direction of the store. But instead of going straight there, she made a sharp turn and rode into the gravel parking lot of the apple orchard. The lot was packed with cars. Kids in winter coats skipped out through the gates, followed by their parents carrying wicker baskets full of shiny red apples.

Jaclyn picked up a basket from the front entrance.

A woman wearing a vest dotted with apple-shaped patches greeted her. "Welcome! Are you here to learn how to make apple pie?"

Jaclyn laughed. "I already know how to do that. I'm here to . . ." Jaclyn thought for a moment. She couldn't exactly explain the real reason she was there. "Pick some apples for my teachers."

The woman smiled. "What a sweet little girl!"

Jaclyn beamed. She marched into the orchard and looked up at the trees. The branches were heavy with apples, but there wasn't a rotten one in sight. She zigzagged through rows and rows of apple trees, the dry leaves crunching beneath her feet. The sun had almost set, turning the sky fiery orange. She would have to head back soon. If she wasn't home by dark, her parents would probably never let her leave the house again.

She reached the far end of the orchard, away from the crowds. There was no one else around. It was eerily quiet. She fastened the top button of her purple cardigan and shivered. Even here, every tree was dotted with plump, ripe apples. She was just about to turn back when a strange buzzing sound cut through the silence. At first, she thought it might have been a beehive, but as she wandered toward it she saw what was really making the sound: flies. They were swarming around a small, sickly-looking tree with a knotted trunk. The tree was surrounded by a low chain-link fence. There were only a few apples on its branches, and all of them looked rotten.

Jaclyn hopped over the fence. She swatted away the flies and plucked the mushy apples from the tree until the branches were bare.

On the way out, the woman in the apple vest spotted her again. "Did you find enough apples for all your teachers?"

Jaclyn nodded. "Can I ask you a question?

What happened to that tree way in the back? The one behind the fence."

The woman looked taken aback. "Oh . . . no one ever notices that tree. It's been here forever. No one can figure out why it grows such rotten apples. Every time we cut it down, it just grows back. Stubborn little tree." She shrugged. "Eventually we put up a fence. It's not the best solution, but we had to do something. You know what they say—one bad apple spoils the bunch!"

Jaclyn thought for a moment. "Why don't you just pull it up at the roots?"

"Hmm. That's not a bad idea."

As Jaclyn left, the woman noticed her basket, which was filled to the brim with soft, putrid apples. She shook her head. "That girl must really hate her teachers."

Jaclyn raced back home. She gave her parents the milk and then went up to her room with her chemistry set and the bushel of bad apples.

She closed and locked her door, and then put on her safety goggles, her lab apron, and her yellow rubber gloves. Then she got to work, following the formula exactly, taking great care to measure every ingredient accurately. She squeezed the juice from the apples, then strained out the mush. She picked out the seeds and plucked the stems, then ground them down with a mortar and pestle. She combined everything in her biggest beaker—the formula had produced much more than she expected. Then she heated it to exactly one hundred and sixty-eight degrees, the final step of the instructions. The pale-yellow mixture began to bubble. Then it changed color to a deep bluish black, like a liquid bruise. She poured a few drops into a test tube. She held the tube up to her nose. It smelled like a dumpster on a hot summer day.

"What am I doing?" she said to herself.

She had spent hours searching for rotten apples and concocting a potion that she'd found in the lab of a dead mad scientist! And now she was about to *drink* it?

There was a sharp knock on the door. Startled, Jaclyn dropped the test tube. It shattered on her desk. The liquid bubbled on the wooden surface, then exploded in a cloud of dark-blue gas right into Jaclyn's face. The awful smell coated her nose. She could taste the bitterness on the back of her tongue. She gagged.

There was another knock on the door.

"Jaclyn?" her mother called.

Jaclyn coughed. "One second!" She wiped her face with her apron, then looked around for some way to hide the mixture. She grabbed an empty plastic water bottle from the trash can, poured the rest of the Perfection Potion inside, and stuck it in her desk drawer. She ran and opened the door. "Hi, Mom."

Her mom peered into the room. "Still working on your science project? Be careful. It won't be easy to clean lava out of the carpet."

"I will."

Jaclyn's mom scrunched up her nose. "It

smells terrible in here. Are you sure you cleaned out Charles's cage?"

"Yes, Mom."

Mom's face softened. "Get some rest. I know today was hard. After a good night's sleep, I'm sure you'll feel like a brand-new person."

CHAPTER SIX
A Brand-New Person

When Jaclyn woke up the next day, the first thing she saw was Charles's cage. She looked at the balled-up socks inside and her stomach twisted with guilt. After school, she would look for him. She just hoped that he was okay.

She got out of bed and rubbed her eyes. It had been a fitful night of sleep with a lot of weird dreams about eating expired food. The odor of rotten apples still lingered in her nose and the acrid taste clung to her throat—even after she'd brushed her teeth twice. She felt foolish for making the Perfection Potion, and vowed not to mention it to Paige and Fatima. It was just too ridiculous. But way in the back of her mind, she couldn't help but wonder—*what if it worked?*

She biked to school and arrived at 7:55 a.m., as she did every day. Just early enough to be punctual, but not so early that she was wasting time waiting for the doors to open. As she walked inside, she saw two sixth graders seated at a folding table topped with freshly baked brownies.

"Hey, Jaclyn!" said Todd Feldhusen in a nasally voice. Todd lived down the street from Jaclyn. He would often knock on her door, selling candy bars or wrapping paper, trying to raise money for one crazy project or another.

"Hi, Todd," said Jaclyn. She turned to Todd's friend. "And you're Davis, right?" She prided herself on knowing the name of every kid in school.

"That's right. You want to buy something from our bake sale?" asked Davis, polishing his glasses on his T-shirt.

"Why are you having a bake sale?" said Jaclyn.

"We're raising money to start a bird-watching club!" said Davis, proudly showing her a giant book of exotic birds.

"Yeah! Bird Buddies!" said Todd.

They high-fived each other, then did a little dance, flapping their arms like wings. It was the most excited anybody had ever been about bird watching.

"What do you need the money for? Binoculars?" asked Jaclyn.

Todd arched his eyebrow. "To buy a bird. *Obviously.*"

"Bird watching is much easier when it's your own bird," added Davis.

"Okay . . . well, good luck."

She gave Todd and Davis a dollar, took one of the brownies, and headed toward her homeroom. That's when she spotted Darcy Lithgow at the water fountain. There was a bright pink pin on her jacket that said *Happy Birthday to Me!*

Jaclyn froze. The cookies. She had been so busy making that stupid Perfection Potion that she had totally forgotten to make a new batch of Grandma Hyde's Chocolate Delights for Darcy's birthday! This was a full-blown emergency! What would Darcy think? What would her classmates say? What would her homeroom teacher do? They would all be so disappointed! The thought of it gave her butterflies in her stomach—big angry butterflies. She had to find a way to fix this mess!

She looked back at Todd and Davis. They were flipping through the book of exotic birds.

"What if we bought a gold-spotted pheasant?" Todd said excitedly. "Or a horned owl?"

"I'm just going to throw a crazy idea out

there," said Davis. "Have we considered a chicken?"

All of a sudden, Jaclyn was overwhelmed by an extraordinarily strange feeling. Her bones ached. Her joints cracked. She glanced down at her hands and was horrified to see that they didn't look like her hands at all. They were smaller. Bonier. With jagged, yellow fingernails. Slowly, she took a step toward Todd and Davis. And then another. But she didn't know why. She wasn't in control of her own body. It was like she was a marionette at the mercy of an invisible puppeteer.

As if in a trance, she quietly approached the folding table. While the two sixth graders eyed the bird book, she reached out and snatched their entire tray of brownies.

What am I doing? she thought. But she was unable to stop herself.

Before Todd or Davis noticed she was there, Jaclyn spun around and sprinted down the hall. She couldn't believe what was happening. She'd never done anything like this. She knew she should put the brownies back—she *wanted* to put the brownies back. But a mysterious force pushed her forward, all the way to homeroom.

The next thing Jaclyn knew, she was standing at the front of her homeroom class.

"Brownies?" Mr. Hanh's voice gave Jaclyn a jolt. She looked down at her hands. They were back to normal. It felt like the puppet strings had been cut and she was in control of herself again.

Mr. Hanh continued, "I was expecting your world-famous Chocolate Delights."

Jaclyn blinked. "Uh . . . surprise!"

Mr. Hanh grinned. "Jaclyn, we can always count on you!"

Jaclyn sat down at her desk in between Paige and Fatima. The whole class sang "Happy Birthday" to Darcy while Mr. Hanh passed out the brownies.

Paige turned to Jaclyn, amazed. "When did you even have time to make these?"

Jaclyn was still having trouble finding her words. "I . . ."

"We know," said Fatima, smacking her on the back. "You can do anything. You're Jaclyn Hyde."

Mr. Hanh passed out brownies to the back row, including Shane Zeigler. Mr. Hanh had barely turned his back when Shane pounded his fist on his desk, crushing the brownie. "Mr. Hahn, somebody crushed my brownie. Can I have another one?"

Mr. Hahn let out a deep sigh. "Shane, *you* crushed your brownie. So no, you can't have another one."

"Whatever." He shrugged. "I don't want any of Jaclyn's brownies anyway. They look like clumps of dirt."

"Well, they taste delicious," said Mr. Hanh, helping himself to seconds. "If only everyone could be like Jaclyn Hyde. Although that wouldn't be good for my waistline," he chuckled. He turned to Jaclyn. "You really are a perfect student."

Jaclyn smiled weakly, but her mind was racing. Had the Perfection Potion somehow made her steal the brownies?

Jaclyn felt a ball of paper hit the back of her head. She picked it up from the floor and smoothed it out on her desk. Beneath smudges of chocolate there were three words: "You're. Not. Perfect."

She turned around. Shane sneered at her and waved with his chocolate-stained hand.

CHAPTER SEVEN
Carved Up

After homeroom, Jaclyn wandered the halls, racked with confusion. She couldn't piece together what had happened. It was like trying to make sense out of a dream. She felt terrible about taking the brownies. She figured she would have to hold her own bake sale to pay Todd and Davis back, or else just buy them a bird. But she had no idea where to get a gold-spotted pheasant, or even a live chicken.

As she reached the locker hallway, Paige tapped her on the shoulder.

"Are you okay? You don't look so good."

"Yeah," said Fatima. "You look like Paige did the day she ate two ham sandwiches before the cross-country meet."

Paige grimaced. "I was really hungry. . . . It was a terrible mistake."

Jaclyn started to unlock her locker. "I think *I* made a terrible mistake—"

Just then, they heard Miss Carver's voice at the other end of the hall. "WHAT IS THIS MESS?!"

Miss Carver was standing at Zeke Trimble's locker. Zeke was the smallest eighth grader in the school, and the baggy turtleneck he wore made him look even smaller. He cowered in front of Miss Carver.

"School rules state that all lockers must be clean and tidy! This is neither clean *nor* tidy!" Miss Carver shouted, her face the color of an undercooked steak.

Zeke's locker was bursting with crinkled papers, piles of textbooks with dog-eared pages, half-sharpened pencils, and capless markers.

"W-w-well," he stuttered. "I tried my best to keep it clean, Miss Carver!"

"Tried?! More like FAILED! Don't ever *try* anything again because clearly it's a waste of your time and mine! You want to keep this locker clean? Here." She reached into the locker and swept everything out. All of Zeke's belongings landed on the ground with a loud clatter. A warped gray eraser bounced across the tiled floor. "Now it's clean."

The rest of the students stood frozen, their eyes glued to Zeke.

Miss Carver whipped around. Her long gray braid hit Zeke in the face. "Everyone open your lockers this instant!"

All the kids within earshot ran to their lockers.

Miss Carver approached Tara Satriale, who was fumbling with the lock like a nervous bank robber trying to open a safe.

"It's a locker combination, not rocket science!" Miss Carver shouted.

"Yes, Miss Carver!" Tara squeaked. The lock finally sprang open.

Miss Carver staggered backward, holding her nose. "Good Lord! Did something die in there?!" She swept all the books out onto the floor next to Zeke's. Then she fumbled around in the back corner and pulled out a brown banana peel.

She bent down so she was eye to eye with Tara. "What is this?" She sneered, angry flecks of spit flying from her mouth and landing on Tara's glasses.

"Um . . . it's a banana peel?" Tara said meekly.

"Were you saving it for later?!" Miss Carver shrieked, and dropped the banana peel onto Tara's head.

Miss Carver made her way down the hall, dumping out the contents of every locker. "Pencil shavings!? Old socks!?" She pulled a notebook out of Hunter Seagram's locker. "What is this?"

"Poetry," said Hunter.

Miss Carver flipped through the pages. "You call this poetry?! IT DOESN'T EVEN RHYME!" She ripped out the pages and tossed them in the air like confetti.

She looked inside Fatima's locker. "I've never seen so many pens in my life!"

"I'm a journalist. I always need something to write with," Fatima explained.

"Oh really?! How's this for breaking news?" Miss Carver grabbed a fistful of Fatima's pens and snapped them in half, spraying ink every-where.

Miss Carver stomped down the hall, emp-tying locker after locker. She reached Paige, whose locker was stuffed with gym clothes. Miss Carver pulled out a pair of cleats. "What are these? Shoes?!"

"They're for soccer practice—"

"This is a locker, not a walk-in closet! You

want to bring extra shoes to school? Wear them on your hands!" She stuffed the shoes onto Paige's hands, and then continued down the hall in a rage. "I didn't know I was running a school full of pigs! Does my name tag say barnyard principal?!"

"You're not wearing a name tag," said Darcy.

Miss Carver pounded her fist against the wall. "That was a rhetorical question! Every single one of these lockers is disorganized, disgusting, and a disgrace." She pointed at the students. "Just like every single one of you."

Then she reached Jaclyn's locker. When she swung it open, she was faced with the tidiest locker in the history of middle school. Somehow Jaclyn had managed to both color coordinate and alphabetize her textbooks. The pencils, each sharpened to the exact same length, were laid neatly inside a pencil box. Her notebooks were stacked according to her class schedule. There was even a pine tree–shaped air freshener hanging on the inside of the door.

Jaclyn smiled sweetly at Miss Carver, hoping she would be pleased that at least one student had followed the rules. Instead, it seemed to make her even angrier.

"What are you trying to do?" she yelled, a vein bulging above her eye. "Make a fool of me?!" She dumped everything out of Jaclyn's locker. She ripped the air freshener off the door, threw it on the floor, and jumped on it. "Stop acting like you're better than the rest of them. You're not." She turned to face the students. "Congratulations. You've all lost your locker privileges for the rest of the year."

She pointed all the way to the end of the hall where Zeke was trying to disappear into his oversized turtleneck. "And you can all thank that little pip-squeak—Zeke Trimble!" She turned and stomped away into her office.

Jaclyn was so busy gathering the contents of her locker and trying to arrange them neatly in her backpack that she didn't get a chance to tell Paige and Fatima about what had happened that morning. They rushed off to Spanish class, while Jaclyn headed to art.

She sat down at her station in front of the painting she had been working on all week. The assignment was to paint a picture of a vase full of sunflowers. There was a real vase full of sunflowers on a stool in the middle of the room for the students to use as a model. Jaclyn mixed her paints together, trying to make the most realistic yellow for the petals as the rest of the class filed in, their backpacks much heavier than before.

Jaclyn was finding it hard to concentrate. She kept thinking about the brownies, and how strange her hands had looked when she'd taken them. And then there was Miss Carver. Every time she had one of these outbursts, Jaclyn always got lumped in with everyone else. It was like all her hard work didn't matter at all.

At least she wasn't the one who'd set her off. Poor Zeke was going to have a hard time getting over this one. This wasn't the first time

Miss Carver had punished everybody because of one person's mistake. In fact, it had happened to most kids in the school at one time or another. They even had a name for it: "Getting carved up." Paige had fallen victim to Miss Carver's wrath in seventh grade. During swim practice, she had accidentally splashed Miss Carver as she walked by. In retaliation, Miss Carver chained the doors to the pool shut. Since then, the pool had sat unused, collecting algae.

Everyone always said getting carved up was unavoidable, but Jaclyn still believed that she could win her over. Upon reflection, she thought, maybe her pencils could have been sharper. Or maybe they were too sharp. She would have to investigate later.

For now, she had to focus on painting these sunflowers. At the completion of each project, the art teacher, Ms. Bicks, chose one student's work to hang up on the wall in a special frame that said *Star Artist of the Week*. Ryan Knowles, a quiet boy with sandy hair and serious brown eyes, had won so many times that the running joke was that Ms. Bicks might as well rename it "the 'Ryan Knowles Painting of the Week' Frame."

As the yellow started to come together on Jaclyn's palette, she thought that maybe—just maybe—she had a chance to win this week.

But then she heard Marina squeal from across the room. "Ryan, that's amazing!"

Jaclyn saw Marina leaning on the table next to Ryan's painting. The sunflowers looked more like sunflowers than the actual sunflowers. They were practically blooming off the canvas! Jaclyn sighed. There was no way she could ever make a painting that good.

She walked to the back of the art room to refill her water cup. She poured out the murky liquid, and as she watched it swirl down the drain, she thought about how much she'd love to be star artist just once. After the week she'd had, it would mean a lot. She was about to turn on the tap when—it happened again. The aching bones.

The cracking joints. She felt herself losing control. The invisible puppet strings were back. But this time, the puppeteer was even stronger. Without knowing why, she walked over to the wall of art supplies. She reached out and grabbed a jar of paint thinner. Her hands were even more grotesque now than they had been when she'd taken the brownies. Wiry hair sprang from knotted knuckles. Her nails were yellower and sharper than before. She poured the paint thinner into her water cup and made her way over to Ryan's station. She felt like she was trying to steer a plane that was heading for the side of a mountain, but it was on autopilot. While Ryan was talking to Marina, Jaclyn switched out his water cup for the cup full of paint thinner.

Jaclyn couldn't say how long it was exactly before she snapped back to normal. It was Ryan's voice that did it.

"My sunflowers!" he shouted. It was the loudest he had ever spoken. Yellow paint dribbled down his canvas. It mixed with the blues and browns of the vase and then dripped into a muddy brown puddle on the floor.

Jaclyn squirmed in her seat but couldn't bring herself to speak up. She looked down and saw that her hands were back to normal. The only yellow on her fingernails was from paint.

Ms. Bicks ran over to Ryan. "Oh, dear! What happened here?"

Ryan ran his hand through his thick blond hair. "I don't know," he said solemnly.

Ms. Bicks smelled his water cup and recoiled from the chemical odor. "Oof! You covered your entire canvas in paint thinner."

Ryan looked completely dumbfounded.

Ms. Bicks turned to the class. "Let this be a lesson to all of you. All the natural talent in the world won't save a sunflower from paint thinner. Now, look at this one." She picked up Jaclyn's painting. "It's a perfectly nice painting *and* she took excellent care of it. Looks like we'll have a new star artist this week."

CHAPTER EIGHT
I'm Jackie!

"**Who's ready** for hot cider?" called Tanya, the cafeteria cook, as she opened the double doors to the lunchroom. The students formed a line, buzzing with excitement. Each year, the second week of October was known as Hot Cider Week at Fog Island Middle School. It was a tradition created by the old principal, Mrs. Goodman, to make the dreary autumn a little cozier. It was the one week of the year when the weird smells of the cafeteria were masked by fresh apples and mulled spices. Even the teachers got into the spirit—except for Miss Carver, who always ate lunch alone in her office no matter the season.

Paige and Fatima brushed past the line and sat down at their usual table. Paige was allergic to apples. They made her lips itchy and her tongue swell. And Fatima thought that waiting in a long line for hot juice was absurd.

Tanya stood behind the counter, which was lined with paper cups. She sloshed a ladleful of cider into each cup. Everyone was allowed one serving.

"Yes!" cheered a seventh grader as he grabbed a cup of cider. He downed it all in one gulp before he'd even left the line. "Why did I do that?" he said, his voice full of regret.

Paige looked at all the kids waiting eagerly in line and sighed. "I'm missing out."

"Trust me, you're not missing out on anything," said Fatima. "This is all just a ploy by the Fog Island Orchard to sell more apples."

"But it smells so good."

Fatima rolled her eyes. "I don't see what the big deal is. Haven't they ever heard of hot chocolate?" She pointed to Paige's sandwich bag. "Don't throw that out, by the way. I'm collecting extra props for the big Trash Beach scene in the musical."

There was only one beach on Fog Island. Its official name was Pogwilly Beach but it was known to the locals as Trash Beach because it was always covered in garbage. For a long time, this phenomenon went unexplained. No matter how many times the beach was cleaned, more garbage always appeared. Finally, a team of researchers had determined that the ocean currents flowed in such a way that they pushed all the debris from the surrounding waters straight to the beach. Anything that fell from the Fog Island Ferry or any fishing boats between Fog Island and the mainland ended up on Trash Beach.

Paige gave Fatima her sandwich bag. "Haven't you filled three trash bags already?"

"It's still not enough," said Fatima. She loved that Trash Beach made Fog Island unique in its own smelly way. That's why she'd decided to set the act one finale of the musical there, with the actors surrounded by algae-filled coffee cans and soggy plastic bags.

As Paige handed Fatima a candy-bar wrapper from her pocket, Jaclyn sat down at the table.

"No cider?" Paige asked. Then she gasped. "Does it make your tongue fat, too?"

"There's no time for cider!" said Jaclyn. "I have to tell you something really important—"

Fatima interrupted, "We already heard you're star artist of the week."

"No, not that!" Jaclyn said sharply. "Well, yes that, but—here's the thing. I didn't earn it."

"Give yourself some credit." Fatima smiled. "I heard your sunflowers were spectacular."

Jaclyn was starting to get frustrated. "Will you listen to me?"

She was interrupted by Tara Satriale, who still had little brown bits of banana in her hair from when Miss Carver had dropped the peel on her head. "Hey, Paige, has anyone asked you for your cider yet?"

It was common knowledge throughout the school that Paige never drank the apple cider, so there were always kids vying for her serving.

"Actually, you're the first today," said Paige, taking a bite of her PB&J. "Go for it."

"Thanks, Paige!" Tara hopped back in line for a second cup of cider.

Jaclyn leaned in closer to Paige and Fatima. "Guys, seriously, there's something really weird going on—"

"Ex-excuse me," said Zeke, edging up to their table. His backpack, now stuffed with all the contents of his locker, stuck out way behind him. In combination with his turtleneck it made him look like, well, an actual turtle. "Fatima, I'd like to submit a request for your cider," he said.

It was also common knowledge that Fatima never drank her serving of apple cider, but she was much more demanding about who got hers than Paige was.

Fatima rested her chin on her hands. "State your case."

Zeke looked down at the floor. "I know I ruined everyone's day by getting their locker privileges revoked, but when I picked up my cider I accidentally squeezed the cup too hard and it spilled all over me." He held up his arm. His sweater sleeve was soaking wet.

"Okay, okay." Fatima held up her hand. "You can have the cider."

Zeke's face lit up with joy. "Really? Thanks!" He ran off.

"What can I say? I felt bad for the guy," said Fatima. "We've all been carved up by Miss Carver at one point or another."

Last year, Miss Carver shut down the school newspaper for the entire spring semester because Fatima was doing a story about the cafeteria food and she asked too many questions about the mixed-meat medley.

By now, Jaclyn was so anxious that she was digging her fingernails into the wooden grooves of the lunch table. Before anyone else could interrupt them, she blurted out a little too loudly, "I stole the Perfection Potion formula, and then I made it!"

Fatima stared at her. "You did?"

"Perfection Potion?" asked Paige, cramming the last piece of her sandwich into her mouth.

"We found a formula in Dr. Enfield's lab," Fatima explained. She turned back to Jaclyn. "You actually made it?"

Jaclyn nodded. "A whole bottle of it. It's in the desk drawer in my bedroom."

"Wait a minute," said Paige. "You're telling me that you have a potion that makes you perfect, and it's just sitting around in your bedroom?"

Before Jaclyn could answer, Marina approached them.

She sat on the edge of the table. "Hey, ladies! Quick question. Jaclyn, I noticed that you didn't have any cider today, and I was wondering if you'd be willing to give your cup to Ryan. He's having a really bad day." She pointed to Ryan, who was sitting at a table by himself, his knees to his chest, rocking back and forth.

Jaclyn felt terrible. "Of course he can have my cider," she said.

"Thanks, Jaclyn. You're the best."

As Marina sashayed off, Jaclyn heard a grunt of disgust behind her. She hadn't noticed that Shane was sitting at the next table this whole time. He held up two soggy green beans on either side of his head to look like pigtails.

"I'm Jaclyn Hyde," he said in a singsong voice. "I'm so great. I'm the most perfect girl in the world. Here, take my cider." He tossed the beans down on his plate. "Give me a break."

Jaclyn couldn't hold her tongue any longer. "Why have you always had it out for me?"

Shane blinked back at her in surprise. "I haven't *always*—"

"Ever since third grade, when you broke my flamingo!"

"When *I* broke your flamingo? I—" Shane let out a huff. "Never mind. Forget it." He picked up his lunch tray and stormed off.

Jaclyn threw up her hands. "I don't get it. What did I ever do to him?"

"Just ignore him. He's a pea brain," said Fatima. "Actually, that's an insult to peas."

"And your pigtails don't look anything like green beans," added Paige.

Fatima leaned in. "So what happened with the Perfection Potion? I need details."

Jaclyn told Paige and Fatima all about the rotten apples picked fresh from the tree, and how she had broken the test tube and gotten a big stinky whiff of the potion right before bed. Then she told them about stealing the brownies and ruining Ryan's painting, and how her hands had looked like they were someone else's. "It's like I'm turning into a completely different person!" she said. "And this person is making me *look* perfect, but . . . not like I expected."

When she finished speaking, she was met with

stunned silence. "You don't believe me," she said.

"It's not that we don't believe you!" said Paige, trying to sound encouraging. "It's just that . . ." She searched for the right words. "You sound crazy."

Fatima jumped right in. "What Paige is trying to say is, you sound . . . not . . . sane."

"But it's true!" said Jaclyn.

Fatima took a deep breath. "We get it. You didn't want to let Darcy down on her birthday, so you took the brownies."

"But it wasn't me!" Jaclyn protested.

"Jaclyn, you can tell us. It's okay. We're your best friends," said Paige. "I once stole a toothbrush from my dentist's office."

Fatima shook her head. "Paige, they give those out for free."

"Really? Hmm. I guess I haven't stolen anything."

"What about the painting?" said Jaclyn. "I would never ruin somebody else's artwork."

Fatima raised her eyebrows. "Really? Not

even so you could be star artist of the week? You've been obsessing about it since September."

"But what about the weird monster hands?!" said Jaclyn.

Fatima looked at Jaclyn's hands. "They seem normal to me. Listen, you've been under a lot of pressure lately, between the science fair and the musical, not to mention losing Charles. Have you considered that this is all in your head?"

"Yeah, stress can make people crazy," said Paige. "Last year during the state championship, my soccer coach threw a grapefruit at the referee."

Jaclyn slumped down in her chair. "Maybe you're right."

Paige stood up and threw her backpack over her shoulder. "I wish I had some Perfection Potion," she joked. "I am *not* ready for the history test next period."

"The test!" Jaclyn shouted. "I totally forgot!" She stood up so quickly that her chair fell over.

"Jaclyn, calm down," said Fatima.

But Jaclyn wasn't listening. "What am I

going to do? I haven't studied at all! This is a complete disaster! I'm going to fail! My life will be over!" Then, it hit her. Hard. The complete loss of control, like she was in the back seat of her own brain and someone else was driving. Everything around her looked fuzzy. She blinked her eyes back into focus and saw that Paige and Fatima were staring at her, their jaws nearly on the floor.

She stood up to run away, but before she could take a step, they each grabbed one of her arms and pulled her out of the cafeteria. Fatima threw her leather jacket over Jaclyn's head so she looked like a celebrity trying to avoid the paparazzi. They smuggled her down the hall and ducked into the bathroom. A sixth grader was standing at the sink.

"Out!" Fatima snapped.

"But I didn't finish washing my hands!" said the sixth grader.

"Washing your hands does nothing! It's all a myth," Fatima lied. "Now, get out!"

The sixth grader scampered away.

Fatima tore the jacket off Jaclyn's head and pointed at the mirror. "Look."

Jaclyn stared at her reflection. But staring back at her was not Jaclyn Hyde. It was someone else entirely. Her hair was frayed and stringy, like her pigtails had been zapped in the microwave. She was short and shrunken; her cardigan hung awkwardly on her bony shoulders. She had a sharp, scowling face and a furrowed brow that cast a shadow over her reptile-green eyes. She held up her hands, which were gaunt and knobbly.

Paige backed up against a stall, hyperventilating. "What the—how did—" She gulped. "Fatima, help!"

Fatima didn't move. "Who are you?" she whispered.

The girl grinned. In a raspy voice that seemed to scrape its way out of her throat, she replied, "I'm Jackie!"

She pushed Fatima out of the way and bolted out of the bathroom.

CHAPTER NINE
Baby Spiders

Jackie ran down the empty hallway, cackling loudly. She felt like a bird that had just escaped its cage. She turned the corner into the locker hallway. She noticed that Miss Carver had cut off the old locks and replaced them with new ones, so the students could never use the lockers again.

Fatima and Paige chased after Jackie.

"Jaclyn, wait!" Fatima called out.

Jackie stopped in her tracks. She whipped

around and put her hand up to her ear. "I'm sorry. Jaclyn can't come to the phone right now," she taunted. "Try again later!" Then she grabbed the nearest trash can and flipped it over. Garbage spilled out onto the floor. Her face lit up with delight. She turned and took off at full speed again.

Paige and Fatima ran after her. Fatima slipped on a half-empty carton of milk and fell to the floor. "Gross!" she exclaimed.

As Paige helped her to her feet, they heard Jackie's voice from up ahead. "Don't cry over spilled milk!"

Lunchtime had just ended and the students were starting to file out of the cafeteria.

"We can't let anyone see her like this," said Fatima.

"I wish I hadn't see her like this," said Paige. "It's the middle of the day and I'm already having nightmares."

They turned the next corner just in time to see Jackie duck into the library.

"There she is," said Fatima.

Fatima and Paige sprinted into the library, which was totally empty. It was eerily quiet—even for a library. They didn't see Jackie anywhere.

"Jaclyn?" Paige called out.

Silence.

Fatima cleared her throat. "Jackie?"

Nothing.

"She did come in here, right?" said Fatima.

"Fati, look out!" Paige tackled Fatima to the floor as a book whizzed through the air, narrowly missing Fatima's head.

"Ow," said Fatima, sitting up and clutching her side. "My ribs."

Paige brushed herself off. "Sorry. I always wanted to play on the football team."

Jackie popped up from behind the circulation desk. "Don't forget to study!" she screeched. Then she started flinging books like frisbees at the girls. They ducked and covered their heads against the flying hard covers. Jackie grabbed the computer off the desk. "Information overload!" she howled as she threw it with all her strength. Fatima and Paige scattered just in time. It landed between them with a loud crash.

"Jaclyn, get ahold of yourself!" Fatima shouted.

"Okay," said Jackie. She jumped on top of the circulation desk, held on to both of her pigtails and pulled them straight up, stretching her face into a grotesque smile. "How's this?"

"Never mind—let go of yourself!" Paige screamed.

Jackie climbed to the top of the nearest bookshelf. She towered over the girls. She grabbed an armful of books and tossed them into the air just as the doors swung open. Todd and Davis walked in.

"I'm telling you, Todd, they probably have a whole book on chickens!" said Davis.

Then they saw the books flying. Their eyes went wide.

"What's going on?" yelped Davis as a book soared past his head.

"Who cares? Run!" said Todd, grabbing his friend's hand and hightailing it out of there as fast as they could.

Jackie cackled and tossed another pile of books down from the shelf.

"Paige, get her!" Fatima called out from under a chair.

"You get her!" said Paige, holding an over-sized picture book above her head for protection.

"You've seen me in PE. I'm terrible at climb-ing."

Paige groaned. "Fine."

She shimmied up the side of the bookcase and peered over the top.

Jackie smiled at her. "Hi, Paige." She chucked an atlas at Paige's face. "Bye, Paige." Jackie leaped off the bookshelf and crashed to the floor. "Oof, didn't stick the landing." She pulled herself to her feet and raced out the door.

Paige and Fatima staggered out of the library, Paige rubbing the lump on her forehead where the atlas had hit her. The halls were packed with students hustling in all directions toward their next class.

"She's totally lost it," said Paige.

"I just hope we haven't lost *her*," said Fatima.

Paige craned her neck over the crowd. She saw Jackie bouncing between the backpacks, knocking kids over, and moving so fast that no one could see her face. Paige zeroed in on Jackie and charged. She lowered her shoulder and plowed forward, clearing the way. She almost went crashing into Ms. Bicks but spun out of the way just in time.

Fatima stumbled along behind her. "You were right, Paige!" she shouted.

"About what? That Jaclyn lost her mind?" Paige called back.

"No—that you should play football."

They had almost caught up to Jackie when Paige saw her take a sharp turn.

"She went into the science lab," she said.

"Oh, great. Nothing dangerous in there," Fatima replied sarcastically.

At that moment, the door to Miss Carver's office flew open, blocking Paige and Fatima's path. Miss Carver leaped out, her face as purple as an eggplant. "NO RUNNING IN THE HALLWAYS!"

Paige and Fatima skidded to a stop.

"Sorry, Miss Carver!" Paige squeaked. "We were just—"

"Just what? Trying to make it look like I run a school full of animals?" She took a threatening step toward them. The thick stench of vinegar filled their nostrils.

"Just . . . trying to get to history class before the big test," Fatima said, breathing through her mouth.

"I don't want to hear your excuses. You want to run at school, then join the track team," Miss Carver snapped. An idea flickered across her face. "That's right—you're both on the track team, starting now! And I'd better not hear about either of you missing a single practice."

Fatima was horrified. "No, Miss Carver . . . please. I hate running."

"You should have thought about that before you disrespected my rules."

Paige raised her hand timidly. "Actually, Miss Carver, I'm already on the track team."

Miss Carver's lips quivered in rage and somehow, her face became even more purple. "Well, now you're *off* it. NOW GET TO CLASS!" She pointed toward the history room.

Seeing no other choice, Paige and Fatima turned around and trudged off to class.

Jackie looked around the empty science lab. She walked between the tall, black-topped tables, and wandered back to a supply cabinet. She took out a bottle of hydrogen peroxide, shook it, and watched it fizz.

She frowned. "Not enough."

She went over to a Bunsen burner and flicked on the gas. The flame spat upward, almost catching one of her pigtails on fire. "Whoa! Too much."

She turned off the burner. Then she spotted a small plastic terrarium on a shelf by the window. It was full of newly hatched baby spiders. Jackie tapped on the side of the terrarium, and the spiders scurried in all different directions. She smiled. "Just right." She heard footsteps outside the door. She looked up and saw a vent covering an air duct in the ceiling above her.

"Come on, babies." She climbed onto a lab table, reached up, and pulled open the vent. Then, she lifted the terrarium into the air duct before hoisting herself up and closing the vent behind her.

Jackie scooted through the dusty ducts, pushing the terrarium in front of her. She reached another vent and peered down. She was right above Miss Carver's office. Miss Carver was throwing a dart at a board covered in yearbook pictures. The dart hit the bull's-eye, puncturing poor Zeke Trimble's nose.

Jackie crawled over the vent as carefully as she could. She made it to the other side without making a sound. She picked up speed, making her way through the maze of air ducts. As she crept over Mr. Hanh's classroom, she saw Mr. Hanh sitting at his desk. He looked around to make sure no one was watching, then licked the last crumbs off the stolen brownie tray.

"Getting closer!" she whispered to herself with giddy anticipation.

Finally, she reached the vent above the history classroom. The students sat quietly in their seats. The history teacher, Mr. Ellis, placed the test papers facedown on their desks. Fatima was in the back of the room, still catching her breath. Paige was next to her, biting her nails. They both looked like they had just seen a ghost.

Mr. Ellis stopped at Jaclyn's empty desk. He looked around the room. "Has anyone seen Jaclyn? She's never late."

Paige and Fatima turned to each other in a panic. Paige mouthed, *Say something*.

Fatima piped up. "She's not feeling . . . like herself today."

"Oh," said Mr. Ellis. "I hope she feels better soon."

"Oh, she will!" Jackie whispered to herself.

Mr. Ellis finished handing out the tests. He looked at the clock. "Okay, class. Your time starts . . . now."

Up in the air duct, Jackie popped the lid off the terrarium, tipped it to the side, and tapped the bottom. A few baby spiders dropped through the vent. Mr. Ellis felt something on the back of his neck. He brushed it away with his hand.

"What was that?" he muttered.

Confused, he looked up. Jackie flipped the terrarium upside down and shook it like a maniac.

"SPIDERS!" Mr. Ellis screamed as one landed on his eye.

Spiders rained down on the room and scattered everywhere. The class plunged into pandemonium. Some of the kids leaped onto their chairs to avoid the spiders crawling on the ground. Others put their backpacks on their heads to protect against the spiders falling from the ceiling.

"They're in my hair!" Marina wailed, running across the room.

"They're in my hair, too!" shouted Mr. Ellis. He was completely bald, but he did have a thick beard that the spiders probably found quite cozy.

The students ran around in a panic. Someone knocked the globe off Mr. Ellis's desk and it smashed on the ground. Another kid tore the world map off the wall to use for protection.

Terrified, Mr. Ellis tried to brush himself off. "They're poisonous!" he shouted. "They'll eat your flesh!" Neither of these things was true, but then perhaps this was why Mr. Ellis was a history teacher, not a science teacher.

Fatima and Paige looked around at the chaos. They knew Jackie had caused it, but they had no idea how she'd managed to do it.

"Everybody out! Save yourselves!" Mr. Ellis

shrieked. He was the first one out the door. The students stampeded out behind him. As Fatima left, she could have sworn she heard laughter coming from the vent.

As soon as the classroom was empty, Jaclyn transformed back into her normal self. Terrified, she glanced around the dusty air duct and backed away in a daze, holding the empty spider terrarium. Without realizing it, she scooted herself right onto the vent. It swung open beneath her, and she plummeted down onto Mr. Ellis's desk. She looked around, disoriented.

She heard Mr. Ellis's voice down the hall. "This way! Hurry!"

She stood up on the desk, swung the vent closed, then hopped down just as Mr. Ellis arrived with Pete, the school custodian.

"They're in there!" said Mr. Ellis, pointing inside the classroom. That's when he noticed Jaclyn standing dumbfounded in the middle of the room, holding the terrarium. "Jaclyn! I didn't see you come into class."

"I . . . uh . . . ," Jaclyn stammered, sure that she had been caught.

Mr. Ellis gave her a heartfelt look. "And you stayed behind to clean up the spiders. What a perfect student!"

CHAPTER TEN
Not Ready for Human Consumption

After school, Paige and Fatima met up at their usual spot by the vending machine right next to the gym. The selection in the machine was bleak. Earlier in the year, Miss Carver had caught Hunter Seagram shaking the vending machine when his bag of chips got stuck. As punishment, Miss Carver had removed all the buttons for the good snacks. The only options left were no-salt saltine crackers and a toxic-looking soda called Caffeine-Free Diet Blue. Paige pressed both buttons.

"Ugh! How can you eat no-salt saltines?" asked Fatima.

Paige grinned. "What Miss Carver doesn't know is how much salt is in the Diet Blue!" She poured a splash of soda onto a cracker and scarfed it down.

Fatima shuddered. "What are we going to do about Jackie?"

Paige bit her lip nervously. "I don't know. I hope I never see that goblin girl again."

Fatima couldn't help herself. "Well, Paige, I don't know if she's technically a goblin—"

"You know what I mean!"

Jaclyn poked her head around the corner "Hey. It's me," she said softly. She was back to her regular self. Her hair no longer looked like she'd been shocked by an electrical socket. Her eyes had changed back from green to brown.

But Paige was still skeptical. "Prove it," she said, shielding herself behind the vending machine.

"Look," Jaclyn said, unzipping her backpack. "I organized all my textbooks alphabetically based on the author's hometown."

Fatima nodded. "It's her."

Paige wrapped up Jaclyn in a big hug.

"I'm so sorry, guys," said Jaclyn.

"You'd better be!" said Fatima. "I'm on the track team now, and you almost made Paige read a book!"

Jaclyn half laughed and half sobbed. She leaned against the wall and sank down to the floor. "What am I going to do?"

Fatima and Paige crouched down next to her.

"What are *we* going to do?" Paige corrected her.

"Remember when I stormed the mayor's office to get an interview for the paper, and you convinced him not to call security?" said Fatima.

Jaclyn gave a little nod.

"Yeah!" Paige said. "And remember at the

sixth grade dance when I felt weird about being the tallest kid in our grade, so you showed up on stilts?"

"We're going to help you get through this," said Fatima.

"You'd do the same for us," said Paige.

"But this is really, really, really bad," said Jaclyn.

"Lucky for you, you have really, really, really good friends." Fatima grinned.

Jaclyn couldn't help but smile a little.

Just then, Miss Carver's sharp voice crackled through the PA system. "Attention, everyone! Stop speaking this instant and listen to your principal! The school musical premieres this evening at seven p.m. A friendly reminder to all students who are in the musical"—she cleared her throat—"if you miss a single line, if you sing a single note off-key, if you mess up a single dance step, you'll wish you'd never set foot on a stage! You'd better not embarrass me because you do *not* want to see me when I'm angry!

Now, break a leg!" The speaker clicked off.

"Wow," said Fatima. "Coming from Miss Carver, that *was* a friendly reminder."

Jaclyn's eyes widened. "I only have a few hours before I have to be in costume for the musical!"

Paige scratched her head. "If only there was a way to reverse the potion. Like an anti-potion potion!"

"You mean an antidote?" said Fatima.

"What's a dote?" said Paige. "You mean like a dote bag?"

"You're thinking of *tote* bag," said Fatima. "But also, great idea."

"What do you mean?" said Paige.

Fatima zipped up her leather jacket. "We have to go back to Enfield Manor."

"What?! Are you crazy? No way!" said Paige.

"Yes way. If there's an antidote, the formula must be in that notebook we found in Dr. Enfield's desk."

"But what about Lord Creepy with his bag full of murder tools?" said Paige.

"Relax," said Fatima. "He probably won't even be there."

Once again, Jaclyn, Paige, and Fatima found themselves on Cedar Street. As they biked toward Enfield Manor, the fog was so thick it was like they were pedaling through a rain-cloud. They parked their bikes and hid behind a mossy tree a few yards away from the wrought-iron gate. They peered around the tree and saw a figure in the front yard. It was the same man they'd seen inside the house the day before.

"You said he wouldn't be here," Paige whispered.

"I said *probably*," Fatima huffed.

The man reached into his canvas duffel bag and pulled out a rusty metal tool.

"What's he doing?" Jaclyn whispered.

"Shh!" Fatima waved her hand.

The man raised the tool high in the air,

then brought it down to the ground with a *SQUELCH*.

"Oh my god!" Paige squeaked. "He's chopping up a body!"

Jaclyn let out a soft scream.

The man turned. Red liquid dripped down his gloves and onto the ground.

"Is that—blood?!" said Jaclyn.

"Forget it!" Paige whispered. "Jackie can throw as many books at me as she wants. Let's get out of here!"

"Wait," said Fatima. She took a few steps forward.

"Fati, what are you doing? Get back here!" Jaclyn said through gritted teeth.

Fatima moved closer and squinted so she could see through the fog.

Jaclyn and Paige covered their eyes. They couldn't bear to look.

Fatima spun around. "Tomatoes."

"What?" Jaclyn asked.

"He's picking tomatoes."

"Out of a dead body?!" Paige said, horrified.

Fatima sighed. *"No."*

Jaclyn stepped out from behind the tree and looked for herself. Fatima was right. The man wasn't a murderer. He was a gardener.

"Come on. Follow me."

Ever since they had snuck into Enfield Manor, Fatima had been thinking about the article she wanted to write about Dr. Cornelius Enfield. She had scoured the internet for anything she could find—but there was surprisingly little information about him. She figured now was the perfect time to find out more.

Fatima approached the gate and said, "Excuse me, sir!"

"AAAGH!" the man jumped back, dropping his shovel. "You scared the living daylights out of me."

"We scared *you*?" said Paige.

"Not a lot of people come around anymore. I don't know why. There's nothing to be afraid of—except for the occasional oversized rat." He took off his gloves and opened the gate, then extended his hand. "I'm Henry, by the way. I'm the groundskeeper."

The girls introduced themselves, and Fatima told Henry she was working on an article about Dr. Enfield for the *Fog Island Middle School Gazette*.

"I'd be happy to help you out. I suppose I know as much about Dr. Enfield as anyone," said Henry.

Fatima pulled a notebook and pencil out of the pocket of her leather jacket.

"Was he really a mad scientist?" Paige blurted out.

Fatima held up her hand. "Let me handle this." She turned back to Henry. "What kind of science did he do exactly?"

"Chemistry, I suppose. There were always odd sounds and strange stenches coming from his lab. Dr. Enfield probably went through a fire extinguisher every other week. But"—he frowned—"near the end of his life, he became obsessed with one project. He worked on it day and night. It got to the point where he never left the house. I don't even think he slept."

Fatima scribbled in the notebook, trying to keep up. "What was the project?"

Henry rubbed his chin. "Some kind of concoction to make people perfect."

Jaclyn and Paige locked eyes with each other.

Henry continued, "It always seemed like a bad idea to me. You can't squash out your imperfections. It'll drive you crazy."

A chill ran down Jaclyn's spine.

Fatima tapped her pencil on her chin. "Dr. Enfield died five years ago. Why do you still take care of this place?"

"I've worked here for over thirty years," said Henry. "When Dr. Enfield passed away, he left the estate to me."

"You live in that creepy old house?" Paige exclaimed.

"No," Henry chuckled. "I live over there."

Henry pointed to a small guest house behind

the manor. It had stone walls and a red door. The grass surrounding it was dotted with purple and yellow flowers. Warm light glowed in the windows, and wisps of smoke rose from the chimney, dissolving into the fog.

"By yourself?" asked Fatima.

Henry's eyes flickered to the ground. "Now, yes. I used to live there with my wife, Greta." He flipped open his wallet and showed them a picture of a woman with curly red hair and a friendly smile.

Jaclyn recognized the woman immediately from the picture in Melanie's yearbook. "That's Greta Goodman!"

"The old principal?" said Fatima.

Henry nodded. "That's right. She loved Fog Island Middle School—and the students loved her. Why wouldn't they? She had this amazing ability to see the goodness in each and every one of them."

"Well, believe me, we wish she was still around," said Paige.

Henry smiled weakly. "So do I."

"What do you mean?" Fatima asked.

"After she retired, she left Fog Island . . . and me. I found a letter that just said, 'I'm leaving.' I never heard from her again. I never understood why. I thought we were so happy together." He dusted some dirt off his sleeve. "Anyway. I try to keep the place nice. I guess I have this silly hope that one day she might come back."

There was a long silence.

"Listen, girls, I promised myself I would finish picking these tomatoes before supper. If you want to have a look around the house, be my guest. Just be careful."

"Thanks," said Jaclyn.

He winked. "Anything for the students of Fog Island Middle School."

The girls walked up the stone path and into the house.

Jaclyn looked around the sitting room. "Charles?" she called out hopefully. But there was no sign of him.

Fatima gave her a sympathetic look. "We have to get the notebook."

As they walked to Dr. Enfield's lab, Paige said, "That Henry guy is so nice. I can't believe we thought he was a murderer!"

"Well," said Fatima, "if you hang around a creepy old house covered in tomato juice, people are bound to make assumptions."

Jaclyn pulled the dusty notebook out of Dr. Enfield's desk drawer. Paige and Fatima gathered around her as she flipped through the pages. As she looked at the writing more closely, it became clear that the pages were filled with different versions of the Perfection Potion formula. Each formula had one ingredient in common, rotten apples fresh from the tree. Other than that, there were all kinds of different measurements and instructions. All the pages were marked up with X's and question marks. In red ink at the bottom of each page were the words:

Not ready for human consumption.

"Do you see anything about an antidote?" Fatima asked.

"Not yet." Jaclyn flipped all the way to the back, just past the page she had torn out. She found a series of notes scribbled in blue ink.

November 29

The experiment is not going well.

I administered the Perfection Potion to Mouse #1.

Once inside the maze, the test subject changed dramatically in appearance.

Test subject grew larger. Claws sharpened. Tail thickened. Fur became wiry. Eyes turned green. Test subject resembled a monstrous rat.

Over the course of the experiment, test subject did not improve her performance in the maze as expected. She destroyed the maze entirely.

Test subject escaped the lab and has not been seen since.

However, I did find a large hole chewed through my snow boots.

Note: Those were my only snow boots.

Note: My feet are cold.

December 13

The experiment has gotten out of hand.

I have administered the Perfection Potion to multiple mice. They all exhibited the same transformation. They've all become monstrous rats.

With continued observation, I've witnessed an even more unexpected phenomenon. At first, the mice returned to their original physical forms, frequently changing from mouse to rat and back again.

However, all of them eventually became trapped in their altered state. The change seems to be permanent.

Jaclyn's eyes widened. "What if Jackie comes back and . . . never leaves?!"

"I don't even want to think about that," said Paige.

"Wait, look!" Fatima said, pointing to a note at the bottom of the page.

January 4

It pains me to admit that the experiment has failed.

Mouse #23 is the only test subject who has not escaped the lab.

I have discovered that a repeat dosage of the Perfection Potion reverses all the effects.

Mouse #23 has permanently returned to its original state.

Note: I wish I had figured this out before the other test subjects ate all my shoes.

Jaclyn was flooded with relief. "That's it? I just have to take it again?" She smiled. She couldn't believe it was so easy. She had a whole bottle full of the Perfection Potion sitting in her desk drawer at home.

Fatima put her arm around Paige. "That, my friend, is what we call an antidote."

"Cool." Paige nodded. "I still don't get what a dote is, though."

Jaclyn, Paige, and Fatima bounded out of the house. They wanted to thank Henry, but he wasn't outside anymore. They saw through the window of his cottage that he was sitting at a table set for one, looking longingly at the empty chair across from him.

"Wow," said Fatima. "He must really miss Mrs. Goodman."

He glanced up and saw the girls, then gave them a little wave. They waved back.

"Come on," said Jaclyn. "We've got enough time to go home and reverse the effects before the play starts!"

They hopped on their bikes and pedaled as fast as they could to Jaclyn's house. Jaclyn's dad was sitting at his computer.

"Hi, Dad!" Jaclyn said, running right past him.

"Hi, Mr. H!" Paige and Fatima shouted as they whizzed by in a blur.

Jaclyn ran into her bedroom, so excited that she nearly tripped over her own feet. When she opened her desk drawer, she felt like her stomach was being wrung out like a wet washcloth. The Perfection Potion was gone.

CHAPTER ELEVEN
Fog Brain

Jaclyn, Paige, and Fatima rushed down the stairs two at a time.

"Dad!" Jaclyn shouted, skidding to a halt in front of him. "Were you in my room?"

Dad swiveled his chair around to face her. "No. I've been down here all afternoon making this." He showed her a T-shirt that said *Proud Dad of the World's Best Understudy*. "I can't wait for the show tonight."

Jaclyn's face flushed. "Dad, you don't have to come. I'm just the understudy."

"The world's *best* understudy!" he corrected her. "I'm going to get a seat all the way to the side, so I can try to see you backstage. And Paige, I hear you're great as the tree!"

"I'm still working on my line," said Paige. "What is it again?"

"'It sure is foggy out,'" Fatima told her for the hundredth time.

"It sure is," Jaclyn's mom said, walking through the front door. She hung her coat up on the hook. "Girls, shouldn't you be getting ready for the musical?"

"Mom, did you go in my room?" Jaclyn asked.

"No, and frankly there's still an odd smell coming from in there. I think you should give Charles's cage another scrub. Now, are you all set for the big show tonight?"

"Yes, Mom, but listen—"

"You know all your lines, right? And all the

dance steps? And every note to every song? Just in case."

Finally, Jaclyn couldn't take it anymore. "So *nobody* was in my room?!" she shouted at the top of her lungs.

Jaclyn's dad blinked at her a few times. "Well, your science fair partner. What's his name? Shawn?"

Fatima's scowled. *"Shane?"*

"That's right. Shane. He was just here. He said he had to pick up something for the project. He's a very polite young man."

"I didn't know you had another science fair partner," said Mom.

"We don't," said Paige.

A look of panic crossed Jaclyn's face. "We've got to go!"

As they ran out the door, Dad called after them, "See you at the show!"

The girls took off on their bikes as fast as they could go. Shane lived at the end of Paige's street in a house with a big tree in the front yard. It was a cherry tree, a fact that Jaclyn knew all too well because when she went over to Paige's house, she'd often have to ride by while Shane hid in the branches and pelted her with sour cherries. It was as good a reason as any to wear a helmet while biking.

"Let's take the shortcut," Paige called out, turning into the Fog Island Orchard.

"I hope we can find him," Jaclyn said, trying to keep her tires steady on the dirt path.

"Oh, we'll find him," Fatima snarled, "and when we do, his brace-face better brace for my fist!"

"How did he know about the potion?" said Jaclyn.

"He must have been snooping on us during lunch. The little weasel!" Fatima said, weaving through a row of apple trees. "Scratch that. That's an insult to weasels!"

Paige was already biking out of the other side of the orchard. As Jaclyn tried to keep up, she looked over her shoulder toward the fenced-off area where she had picked the rotten apples. She saw something that made her slam on the brakes of her bike. The tree was ripped out of the ground. It was laid next to a tractor, its roots dried and frayed. Jaclyn remembered how she'd suggested to the woman in the apple vest that they dig the tree up at the roots. Apparently, they had taken her advice. She kicked herself for saying anything at all. Now, she could never make more Perfection Potion. She had to get it back from Shane. She gripped her handlebars tight and caught up to Paige and Fatima.

They popped out of the orchard and turned onto Paige's street. They looked around. There was no sign of Shane.

"Oh, no—we missed him," said Jaclyn.

But just then, Shane turned the corner. The Perfection Potion was in the water-bottle holder of his bike, the dark-blue liquid sloshing around as he rode. When he saw the girls, he braked so hard he nearly tipped over.

"We've got you now, you human wart!" Fatima shouted.

"Oh, yeah?" Shane said, turning his bike around. "Come and get me!" He sped off in the opposite direction, the thick fog engulfing him almost immediately.

"Challenge accepted!" yelled Paige. She pedaled off after him at full speed.

"Oh, great." Fatima groaned, clutching her side. "I was really hoping the exercise portion of this day was over."

They raced through town with Shane in the lead, Paige in the middle, and Jaclyn and Fatima bringing up the rear. As they got to the town square, Paige nearly caught up to him. She reached out to grab the potion, while still pedaling at full speed. At the last second, Shane swerved, sending Paige off balance. She crashed into the gazebo in the middle of the square. Shane biked off into the distance.

Fatima and Jaclyn caught up to Paige.

"Are you okay?" said Jaclyn.

"Yeah, it was nothing," Paige said, brushing herself off. "Come on. He's heading toward the Foggy Woods."

"Wait, Foggy Wood or the Foggy Woods?" said Jaclyn.

Foggy Wood was the local lumberyard. The Foggy Woods was the creepy forest on the outskirts of town.

"The Foggy Woods!" Paige shouted in frustration. "Why does everything on this Island have to be named after fog?"

Fatima explained, "Because when the founders landed here, all they could see was fog. It really limited their creativity. They called it 'fog brain.'"

The girls rode to the edge of the Foggy Woods. They slowed down as they entered the forest. Centuries-old trees towered over them, the trunks covered in knots that looked like wooden eyeballs. The dense leaves blocked out nearly all the light from the sky. Green stringy moss hung from the branches like the trees had runny noses. They biked forward as quietly as they could, listening for any sign of Shane. A gray squirrel darted along the ground, and the girls jumped at the rustling sound.

They reached a fork in the road. Jaclyn looked at the two paths, each swallowed by fog. One path went up to Fog Point, a crag of rocks at the edge of the wood that jutted out high above the ocean. The other path wound down to Pogwilly Beach.

"Which way?" said Fatima.

Jaclyn sighed. "I have no idea."

Paige shuddered. "This place is so creepy."

"It's not creepy. It's just foggy," said Fatima.

"Look! There's blue goo coming out of the trees!" Paige said, pointing to a tree on their left.

"What are you talking about?" said Fatima.

Jaclyn walked over to the tree. There was something bright blue on the trunk. But it wasn't coming *from* the tree. It was stuck *on* the tree.

"It's his gum," said Jaclyn.

"He's got to be this way. Let's go," said Paige.

They tore off as fast as they could, but biking up a steep hill wasn't easy.

"Why did he have to go the *uphill* way?" Fatima called from behind.

Finally, the ground leveled off. They picked up speed until they reached Fog Point and skidded to a stop.

Shane was standing at the edge of the rocks, holding the Perfection Potion. He was surrounded on three sides by sheer cliff. Far below, the icy gray waves churned and smashed against the rock wall.

They skidded to a stop.

"Don't come any closer!" he said, dangling the bottle over the cliff.

Jaclyn got off her bike. "Shane, please. Give it back."

"Pretty please, Shane?" he mimicked. "Not so perfect without your precious perfect juice, are you, Jaclyn Hyde? I knew you were a fake. All this time, everyone thought you were so amazing. Ever since kindergarten when you could say your ABC's forward *and* backward."

Paige leaned over to Fatima. "There's a backward version?"

Shane continued, "When I heard you at lunch talking about your little potion, it all made sense. You're a cheat and a liar. You always have been."

"You don't understand," said Jaclyn.

"No, *you* don't understand!" he shouted back, startling all three of them. "Every teacher on this godforsaken island is always bugging me." He took on a high-pitched whiny voice. "'Would Jaclyn do that?' 'Take a page out of Jaclyn's book!' 'Why can't you be more like Jaclyn Hyde?'" He kicked a rock, and it tumbled off the edge of the cliff. "I'm sick of it."

Fatima put her hands on her hips. "What's your plan here, Shane? We've got you surrounded."

"My plan?" He shook the bottle. "I'm going to be the perfect one now. Get ready, Jaclyn. Before you know it, everyone is going to be asking you why you can't be more like that perfect

Shane Zeigler!" He grinned widely.

Just as he was about to open the bottle, Jaclyn blurted out, "It's not going to work."

"Why? Because I'm just *so* imperfect that perfect juice won't work on me?" he scoffed.

"No!" Jaclyn shouted. "Because it's a complex scientific formula that requires precise preparation. You can't just drink it. You have to heat it up to exactly one hundred and sixty-eight degrees. You need a Bunsen burner. You need a thermometer. Did you think any of this through?!"

Shane stared at her, bewildered. Then his eyes cast down to the ground and his face twisted into a furious scowl. "Stupid . . . stupid . . . stupid . . . ," he muttered. He smacked his own forehead. "You are so stupid."

Jaclyn's face softened. "Shane, stop."

"No. Everybody says that I'm dumb. That I always mess everything up. My teachers, my parents, even my little brother. And I guess they're right."

"Come on, Shane, that's not true," said Jaclyn, taking a step toward him.

"Don't act all nice now. It's your fault."

Jaclyn's mouth fell open. "How is it my fault?"

"Everyone has treated me like a screw-up ever since the day you told them I broke your stupid flamingo."

"You *did* break my flamingo. And it wasn't stupid!"

Shane grimaced. "Whatever you say, Jaclyn. I guess I'll never be perfect. But now . . . neither will you."

He tossed the bottle off the cliff.

"NO!" Jaclyn, Fatima, and Paige screamed. They ran to the edge and watched it plummet all the way down until it landed in the frothy waves.

Shane brushed past them and got on his bike. "Don't be late for the musical, losers."

CHAPTER TWELVE
The Moose Is Loose

The last of the Perfection Potion was gone. Jaclyn wished she could go home to her chemistry set and make more, but the tree had been uprooted. There were no more rotten apples. She had no choice but go to the musical and hope that Jackie wouldn't show up. And if she did, Jaclyn worried that she might never turn back into herself. Dr. Enfield wrote in his notebook that all the lab mice eventually became trapped in their altered states. The thought of becoming Jackie forever was almost too much to bear.

From the backstage of the theater, Jaclyn peeked through the curtain. The auditorium was filling up with people. Parents settled younger siblings into their seats. Grandparents readied their cameras. She spotted her mom and dad all the way at the far end of the front row, her dad sporting his homemade T-shirt. Sitting in the center of the front row was Miss Carver. She had a pair of small opera glasses around her neck. She always brought her opera glasses to the student productions, as well as every sporting event, so she could better spot the mistakes.

"Five minutes until places. Everybody circle up," Mr. Collins announced. The cast and crew gathered in a circle backstage. Jaclyn stood next to Marina. They were dressed in the exact same costume, the red checkered pioneer dress. Even with all her other problems, Jaclyn couldn't help but feel jealous that Marina was going to be the only Penny Pogwilly onstage. Fatima stepped in the circle next to Jaclyn, and Paige squeezed in next to Fatima, though it was hard for her to find room with all the leaves sticking out of her arms and legs. Shane skulked over, making sure to stand as far away from the girls as possible.

Mr. Collins began his pep talk. "Okay, my little Fog Islanders, tonight is the big night. You all have worked your foggy little bottoms off for this, and I just know it's going to go off without a hitch. Except for the part when we hitch a wagon to the Fog Island Ferry. That's on you, Zeke."

"Got it!" Zeke Trimble piped up.

"I'd like to give a special shout-out to my coplaywright, Fatima Ali. Without you, *Fog Island: The Musical* wouldn't exist."

Everyone in the circle clapped.

Fatima gave a humble nod. "Well, Mr. Collins, without your songs, *Fog Island: The Musical* would just be *Fog Island: The Factually Accurate Play.*"

"Thank you for saying that." Mr. Collins clasped his hands together. "I do have one more creative suggestion—"

"Oh, no . . . ," Fatima said under her breath.

"Have you considered changing the title to *Fog Island: The* Moose-*ical*?" He held up the moose costume, his eyes full of hope.

Fatima clenched her fists. "Mr. Collins, for the last time, there are no moose on Fog Island."

"Fine, fine. I had to try. It's just such a great costume." He put the costume down. "And one more thing," he said, his tone becoming much more serious. "Miss Carver will be watching our every move tonight, so make sure you do everything as we rehearsed it. No—better than we rehearsed it. Darcy, make sure the sound cues are timed exactly right. Miss Carver isn't going to cut you any slack just because it's your birthday."

"You got it, Mr. Collins," said Darcy.

"And Ryan, run the lights just like we planned. I don't want any artistic interpretations."

Ryan brushed his sandy hair away from his eyes. "The stage is my canvas and the lights are my paint," he said softly.

Mr. Collins looked a little concerned, but he pressed forward. "Shane, you're on the fog machine, so . . . well, I guess it's not a big deal if the fog isn't perfect. Just try not to mess up too much."

Jaclyn looked over at Shane. Instead of his usual smirk, he cast his eyes to the ground, his shoulders slumped. "Okay, Mr. Collins," he said quietly.

"All right, everybody, hands in!" said Mr. Collins. Everybody put their hands in the middle. Paige laid a branch-covered hand on top of the pile. "One-two-three . . ."

"Fog Island: The Musical!" the students all cheered at roughly the same time. Then they scampered off to their places. Paige went off to the corner to practice her one line.

Fatima walked over to Jaclyn. "Are you okay?"

Jaclyn forced a smile. "Yup. I've got everything under control. I'm just going to be the perfect understudy and stay right here in case anyone needs me. I might even get some work done on our science fair project during intermission. I still need to reformulate the lava so it doesn't explode everywhere."

Fatima could see how hard Jaclyn was trying to keep it all together. She put a comforting hand on her shoulder. "Don't worry. We're going to get this all figured out. I've got to get to my seat now. They put me in the front row right next to Miss Carver, so it's going to be a weird-smelling couple of hours for me." She pulled her notebook and pen out of her jacket pocket.

"What's that for?" asked Jaclyn.

"The review for the school paper. Just because I wrote the play doesn't mean I get the night off. And I'm determined to be completely objective." She clicked up the pen and headed for her seat.

As Jaclyn sat down on the frayed couch backstage, Marina approached her.

"Hey, Jaclyn?" said Marina, blinking her big brown eyes.

"Oh, hey," said Jaclyn. "Are you ready for your big solo?"

"I think so. I've been working really, really hard on it. Anyway, I just wanted to say it's been fun rehearsing this play with you. I couldn't have asked for a better understudy. You're so talented. It could just as easily be you out there."

Suddenly, Jaclyn felt bad for ever being jealous of Marina. She really was just trying her best. "Thanks, Marina. You're going to nail it. If you need anything, I'll be here waiting in the wings. Oh, and don't forget your wig! Remember, when the original settlers came to Fog Island, bangs were outlawed."

Marina reached up and felt the top of her head. "Oh my gosh! I almost forgot! Thank you!" She hurried down the hall toward the costume closet.

As soon as Marina turned the corner, Jaclyn felt it happening again. In a matter of seconds, Jackie was back. Her neck bones cracked; her nails sharpened into claws. Jaclyn was no longer in control. She felt like she was locked in a fortress, peering out through Jackie's eyes.

Jackie leaped up from the couch and looked around, careful not to be caught. She saw the brown velvet moose costume crumpled on the ground.

"Come here, moosie!" she hissed.

She stepped into the moose costume and zipped it up. Only her green eyes were visible through the eye holes. She tiptoed down the hallway, giggling quietly to herself. When she got to the costume closet, the door was open. Marina was digging through a box of wigs, humming the notes of her solo. She found the wig she was looking for—blond and ponytailed, just like the real Penny Pogwilly. She was about to put it on when Jackie snatched it out of her hands.

Marina gasped. "What's going on?"

"The moose is loose!" Jackie cackled. Then she ran out of the costume closet and slammed the door behind her. She grabbed a broomstick and shoved it through the door handle, locking Marina inside.

Marina shouted, "Let me out!" But her voice was so muffled by the door that no one could hear her.

Jackie hoofed it back to the tattered couch just as Mr. Collins was finishing up his opening-night speech to the crowd.

"Sit back, relax, and please enjoy *Fog Island: The Musical*!" Mr. Collins announced. The audience applauded, and Mr. Collins went backstage. The lights dimmed. The orchestra played the first few notes of the opening number. The cast took their places onstage.

Mr. Collins looked around and panicked. He clutched his chest. "Where's Marina?" he whispered. "The show is starting!"

And just like that, Jaclyn found herself back

in her own body, wearing a moose costume. She quickly unzipped it and took the head off and ran over to Mr. Collins, determined to tell him what Jackie had just done. "Mr. Collins, I have to tell you something—"

"There's no time! The show must go on!" Mr. Collins whispered. He saw the blond wig in Jaclyn's hands. He grabbed it and put it on her head. "Don't let me down! Who am I kidding? You're Jaclyn Hyde. You'd never let me down!"

"But—" Jaclyn tried.

"Now, get out there!" Mr. Collins gave her a firm shove and she stumbled onto the stage. The curtain rose. The lights went up. The musical began.

CHAPTER THIRTEEN
It Sure Is Foggy Out

One, two, kick, turn, Jaclyn thought as she flawlessly executed every dance step. For the first time, she wasn't hidden backstage; she was under the bright lights. All the hours of practice were really paying off. She hit every note in "This Land Is Fog Land." She nailed the tap dance during the duet "Fog Horns for Sale." She led the entire cast in a showstopping song set in the orchard called "You're the Apple of

My Pie." She could see her parents in the audience, beaming with pride. Even Miss Carver's normally acrid expression was twisted into something that resembled a smile. Jaclyn was a star.

But she had learned in science class that some stars are destined to explode. And that's exactly how she felt as the first act neared its end. During the entire show, all she wanted to do was rush offstage and free Marina from the costume closet, but as the narrator, she had to be onstage for every scene.

The show was quickly closing in on the act one finale, which took place on Trash Beach. During the scene, Penny Pogwilly had a big solo called "A Trash Can Made of Sand." This was the song that Marina had been practicing for months. Jaclyn had to find a way to get Marina out of that costume closet in time for her to have her big moment.

Luckily, Zeke was just starting his ferry-hitching monologue. As he hitched a covered wagon to an old-timey ferry boat, he talked at length about the lonely life of a ferry boat captain in the early days of Fog Island. Jaclyn knew that this was her chance. Even though she was technically supposed to stand with the rest of the ensemble and, according to Mr. Collins's directions, "Listen with your eyes," she knew she could duck away unnoticed.

She ran down the hallway to the costume closet as fast as she could and pulled the broom out from the door handle. She found Marina sitting on the wig box, her head in her hands.

Marina leaped to her feet. "Jaclyn! Thank goodness! I got locked in here by a moose!"

Jaclyn could hear Zeke finishing up his monologue onstage. There wasn't any time to explain. She took off the wig and shoved it into Marina's hands. "Take this! You can still make it in time for your big solo!"

Marina fixed the wig onto her head, overcome with emotion, and gave Jaclyn a hug. "Thank you. You're the best understudy ever."

As Marina ran toward the stage, Jaclyn breathed a sigh of relief. But the relief didn't last long. Jackie was fighting to come back. Jaclyn felt it deep in her bones.

"Oh no . . . ," said Jaclyn.

Within seconds, she had completely transformed.

"Oh yeah!" said Jackie.

She chased after Marina, but by the time Jackie reached the wings, Marina was already stepping onstage. The lights were dimmed while the stage was being set to look like Trash Beach.

Jackie looked around. She spotted a staircase that led to a storage area underneath the stage. She scampered down the steps into the darkness. She pushed past piles of old props and crouched down directly below center stage.

"Don't worry, Jaclyn," Jackie whispered. "I'll get you back in the spotlight before the big solo. Your parents will be so proud. The whole school will be talking about you for years to come. Even Miss Carver will love it!"

Above her, the stagehands pushed the painted ocean background into place and littered the ground with trash. Marina stood on the taped X that marked center stage. Just as the orchestra played the opening notes to "A Trash Can Made of Sand," Jackie pulled the latch on the trap door.

Marina dropped down and landed underneath the stage. It was so dark she could barely see anything when out of nowhere, a pair of knobby hands reached out and grabbed her.

"Give me that!" said Jackie, yanking the wig off Marina's head.

Marina was so shocked that she stumbled backward and tripped over a pile of old prop swords from *The Three Moose-keteers*. Before she could manage to get a word out, Jackie scrambled up onto the stage and pulled the trap door shut.

As the bright spotlight turned on, Jaclyn was back. No one in the audience knew she had ever left. She felt like she had been blindfolded and spun around a million times. She gathered herself just in time to sing the first verse of the solo. She belted out the notes, trying her best to keep from falling apart. How could she possibly fix this? Out of the corner of her eye, she saw Marina stumble into the wings, looking pale as a ghost. As Jaclyn neared the final verse of the song, Shane released a massive blast of fog from the fog machine. Technically, that wasn't supposed to happen until the end of the song, but it was close enough—and it was perfect timing for Jaclyn to run offstage. She plopped the wig onto Marina's head.

Marina stared back at her in utter confusion. "Wh-what's happening?!" she stammered.

"There's no time to explain! Go!" Jaclyn pushed Marina onstage just as the fog cleared. A murmur of surprise spread through the audience. Marina looked stunned. Sure, she had rehearsed for months, but nothing could have prepared her for this.

Jaclyn watched with anticipation, hoping Marina could make it through the end of the song. Shane stood next to her at the fog machine, bewildered.

It was time for the final verse. Marina opened her mouth to sing. That's when Jackie came back. As her bones shriveled and her eyes flickered green, Shane let out a loud scream.

Jackie clapped her hand over his mouth. "Quiet!"

Marina's voice floated through the auditorium. It sounded so beautiful that it made Jackie's skin crawl. She couldn't take it. She completely lost control. She couldn't let Marina outshine Jaclyn like this. She began pulling the rope to close the stage curtain.

"What are you doing?!" Shane yelped.

"Show's over," Jackie spat.

She tugged as hard as she could, feeling the rope burn on her sweaty palms. The students onstage looked around, perplexed. Marina glanced nervously at the curtain but she kept on singing.

Shane grabbed Jackie's arm and tried to pull

her away from the rope. She shook him off and climbed up the edge of the half-closed curtain. As Marina sang the final note of the song, Jackie tugged as hard as she could. The rungs snapped, and the curtain came crashing down. The covered wagon and painted background toppled over. Marina shrieked and fled in fear, along with the rest of the cast. Only Paige stood strong, firmly planted where she was. After all, it was time for her one and only line.

She cleared her throat. "It sure is foggy out!"

The entire audience sat frozen in shock—until Miss Carver broke the silence. "What is the meaning of this?!" She leaped up from her chair and stalked onto the stage. "I have never been so embarrassed in my entire life! You call this a musical?! I call it a tragedy!"

Mr. Collins stepped out onstage. "Miss Carver, this is *not* what we rehearsed."

"An excuse? From the director? How's this for direction?" She pointed at Mr. Collins. "YOU'RE FIRED! I NEVER WANT TO

SEE YOUR FACE AGAIN!"

Mr. Collins let out a sob.

Miss Carver approached the curtain. "Now, let's see who's responsible for this." She flung the curtain aside.

Crouched on the stage in her pioneer dress was Jaclyn.

Everyone in the auditorium gasped.

"Well, well, well. Jaclyn Hyde." Miss Carver's mouth twisted into a wicked smile.

Jaclyn glanced out at the crowd. Her mom looked horrified. Her dad covered his face with his hands. Fatima stood up from her seat in the front row. She locked eyes with Jaclyn. Jaclyn looked back at her helplessly. Then the entire crowd watched Fatima turn and run out of the auditorium. Her parents got up from their seats and chased after her.

Mr. Hanh stood up. "I don't believe it! Jaclyn would never do something like this! Just this morning, she brought fresh-baked brownies to my classroom!"

Todd leaped up from his seat. "Hey! Somebody stole the brownies from our bake sale this morning!"

"Yeah!" added Davis angrily. "And now we can't afford to buy a chicken!"

Ms. Bicks held up her hands. "Let's not get carried away, everyone! Jaclyn is a model student. She's my star artist of the week!"

Ryan Knowles stuck his head out of the light booth. "Wait a minute! Jaclyn was right behind me in art class today when my painting got destroyed. She must have swapped my water cup with paint thinner. I put my soul into those sunflowers!"

Mr. Ellis jumped up and shouted, "I found Jaclyn at the scene of the crime when my classroom got infested with baby spiders. I'm *still* picking them out of my beard!"

The audience broke out into a babble of surprise and disbelief.

Miss Carver sneered at Jaclyn. "I always suspected you were as bad as all the rest of them.

Turns out, you're the worst of all. And you know what they say, one bad apple spoils the bunch." She turned to the crowd. "The Fog Island Middle School theater program is canceled forever! And don't even think about eating any intermission snacks—the snacks are canceled too!" She pointed at Jaclyn. "And you can all thank Jaclyn Hyde."

CHAPTER FOURTEEN
Shoot for the Moon

Dad drove home in stunned silence, while Mom looked back at Jaclyn, her eyebrows knitted with concern. Jaclyn stared out the window, trying to avoid her gaze.

"I don't know where to begin," said Mom. But that didn't stop her from beginning. "I can't believe you would do something like this. I'm worried, Jaclyn. It's so unlike you. What were you thinking?"

Jaclyn struggled to come up with the right words. How could she even try to explain Jackie? She stammered, "It—it wasn't me."

"Well, of course it was you," Dad said, befuddled. "You were the only one underneath that curtain. And what's this about stealing brownies from two sixth graders?" He shook his head. "Those kids just wanted a chicken."

Mom said, "Not to mention sweet Ryan Knowles—"

Dad interrupted, "You poured paint thinner all over his soul."

Mom put her hands to her temples. "And what kind of person dumps baby spiders all over their history teacher?"

"That poor man is going to have to shave his beard now."

Jaclyn shouted in desperation, "I told you, it wasn't me!"

Dad pulled into the driveway and stopped the car abruptly. "Enough. I don't know what's gotten into you, but the least you can do is take responsibility for your actions."

Mom added, "If it wasn't you, then who was it?"

"It was . . ." Jaclyn took a deep breath. "Nobody."

"Unbelievable," said Mom. "Just go to your room."

When Jaclyn got to her room, she found a bouquet of flowers on the bed with a card that said, *You'll always be our star! Love, Mom & Dad.* She felt like a bee had stung her right in her heart. Her parents had never been so upset with her. The whole school thought she was a backstabbing monster. And she kept replaying one moment in her mind: Fatima jumping out of her seat and running out of the auditorium. Fatima had worked so hard to write the musical, and Jackie had ruined her big night. In fact, Jackie had ruined everything. And Jaclyn had a feeling it was only going to get worse.

She opened the rabbit cage and picked up the rolled-up ball of socks that was supposed to look like Charles. She held it close to her chest, curled up on her bed, and fell asleep.

When Jaclyn got to school the next morning, she saw that Todd and Davis were having another bake sale. There was a tray of cupcakes on the table, along with a sign that said "Bake Sale to Earn Back the $ for the Baked Goods Jaclyn Stole."

Jaclyn was mortified. She wanted to give them all the money she had in her wallet. As soon as she took a step toward the table, Todd put his arms protectively around the tray, like a mother bird defending her eggs—not that Todd and Davis would know much about that, since they hadn't been able to buy a bird.

"Stay away, thief!" Davis shouted.

"Yeah!" said Todd. "These are baked *goods*, Jaclyn. They're for *good* people!"

Jaclyn's face flushed red with embarrassment, and she hurried away. She headed toward Mr. Hanh's class for homeroom. On the way, she saw Marina getting a drink from the water fountain.

Jaclyn walked up behind her. "Marina, I'm really sorry . . ."

Marina spun around, water dribbling from her mouth. "AAAGH!" she screamed, and sprinted away.

Jaclyn stood there helplessly. Everyone was glaring at her. She wished she could just disappear. She got to homeroom and noticed right away that Fatima's chair was empty. The slimy knot of guilt in her stomach tightened. She couldn't even apologize to one of her best friends. Luckily, her other best friend was waving her over. As Jaclyn made her way over to Paige, she noticed Shane in the back corner, trying not to look at her. There was no sneer, no mean quip. He just looked afraid.

Jaclyn sat down next to Paige.

"Hi," said Paige. "Are you . . . how are you?"

"Well, I ruined the play and everybody hates me."

"I don't hate you."

"You don't?"

"Of course not! Personally, I was glad the play ended early. I didn't want to stand there for the whole second act. All those tree branches stuck in my hair were really starting to itch. Plus, I got to take home all the intermission snacks." She unzipped her backpack. It was packed to the seams with chips and candy bars. "I'll never have to go to that stupid vending machine again!"

Jaclyn let out a little laugh in spite of herself. "Where's Fati?" she asked.

Paige shrugged. "I tried to call her last night, but she didn't pick up."

Jaclyn bit her lip. "She must be really mad at me."

Paige leaned over and whispered, "If she's mad at anyone, it should be Jackie. She's the one who caused all this, right?"

"I guess so."

Paige looked around to make sure no one was listening. "What are you going to do?"

Jaclyn put her head in her hands. "I have no idea. Move to a desert island and never come back? Or maybe I'll try to launch myself into orbit." She remembered the poster in the guidance counselor's office. *Shoot for the moon,* she thought. *Hopefully you'll miss and end up stuck in outer space forever.*

Mr. Hanh rang the little bell on his desk and the class got quiet.

"Good morning! I hope everyone enjoyed the musical last night. Or the first half, anyway . . ." He gave Jaclyn a look. "The statewide exams are next week. I trust you all will study hard and do your best. As a reminder, cheating and sabotage will not be tolerated. Did you hear that, Jaclyn?"

Jaclyn was taken aback. "Of course, Mr. Hanh."

"You're not going to let tarantulas loose in the testing rooms?"

Jaclyn slumped down in her chair. Now she knew what Shane must feel like all the time.

And it was awful. "No, Mr. Hanh," she murmured.

After homeroom, she made her way down the hallway with Paige through a sea of dirty looks. She stopped in front of the art room. She saw through the window that Ms. Bicks had taken down her painting. The Star Artist of the Week frame was empty. Then they passed the auditorium. The doors were chained shut.

Mr. Collins walked by, carrying a cardboard box filled with a few things from his office, along with his moose costume. "Hello, Jaclyn," he said coldly.

"Mr. Collins, I'm so sorry."

"Me too. I don't know what I'm going to do now that I'm out of a job. I just hope you enjoyed your moment in the spotlight." He took a deep breath. "One more cup of hot cider, and then it's goodbye forever."

As he walked away, Paige could see that Jaclyn was on the verge of tears. "Come on," she said, leading her into the nearest bathroom.

Jaclyn's chest felt tight. She was breathing heavily. She tried to wipe away the tears from her eyes before they fell.

Paige gave her a paper towel. "Don't worry, it's not that bad!" she said.

"Yes, it is!" Jaclyn cried.

"A demon girl made you look like a conniving crazy person in front of the whole school and now she's trying to take over your body. *So what?*" She winced. "Actually, that does sound really bad."

Jaclyn let out a loud sob.

Behind her, the door to the bathroom flew open.

"There you are!" Fatima exclaimed. There was algae stuck in her hair, her jeans were caked in mud, and her leather jacket was dripping with water. She smelled like the inside of a dumpster. "You are *not* going to believe where I've been."

CHAPTER FIFTEEN
Hot Potato

As Fatima sat in the auditorium watching the act one finale of *Fog Island: The Musical*, she wasn't paying attention to the chaos unfolding in front of her. She was barely listening to Miss Carver's shouts of anger as she stormed onstage and revealed Jaclyn beneath the curtain. Fatima was too busy thinking about the chorus of the final song, "A Trash Can Made of Sand":

Everything ends up on Trash Beach,
Even what you thought was out of reach.
The ocean brings the trash to the shore.
Clean all you want; there will always be more.

It was at that moment that Fatima realized what she had to do. Forget the rest of the play; Jaclyn's spectacular flameout was a grander ending than she could have ever written. She had to get to Trash Beach to find the Perfection Potion.

She explained everything to her parents— or, as much as they needed to know—and they drove her straight to the beach. The only light came from Fatima's flashlight and a small sliver of the moon peeking out from the clouds. She sifted through mounds of trash, looking for the nondescript water bottle full of dark-blue liquid. While she was writing the musical, she had read a scientific paper about the currents that funneled all the junk in the water onto the beach. Since Shane had tossed the bottle into the ocean hours earlier, she figured it had to be on Trash

Beach by now. She only hoped she could find it before the waves brought in a new batch of debris that would bury it entirely. At one point she thought she had found it, but it turned out to be a half-drunk bottle of Caffeine-Free Diet Blue. Fatima continued her search, but when an army of raccoons descended on the beach for a late-night snack, she knew she had to call it a night.

As soon as the sun rose the next day, she convinced her dad to drive her back to the beach. Mr. Ali knew that when Fatima had her mind set on something there was no stopping her. He sat on the rocks sipping coffee while his daughter stomped along the soggy sand, kicking away empty cans, looking under plastic bags, and trying unsuccessfully to dodge the incoming waves that crashed onto the shore. All in all, she searched the beach for three hours and twenty-six minutes, got knocked over by nine waves, and was pinched by exactly one cranky hermit crab.

". . ."

"So, long story short," Fatima said, taking off her soaking-wet jacket and cramming it into the trash can next to the bathroom sink, "You owe me a new leather jacket. And"—she reached into her backpack—"I found this." She handed Jaclyn the bottle of Perfection Potion.

Jaclyn and Paige tackled Fatima in a hug.

"You're the best friend ever!" said Jaclyn.

"Yeah!" said Paige. "But you really do smell awful." She took a step back.

Jaclyn sighed with relief. "I thought you left last night because you were mad at me for ruining the play."

"Come on, it's just a play. But I've got to warn you, my review in the school paper is going to be scathing."

Jaclyn laughed. "After all this, that's the least of my problems." She hugged Fatima again. She didn't even care about the garbage smell.

"What are you waiting for?" said Paige. "Drink it!"

But there was one more step. "I just have to heat it up first," said Jaclyn.

The girls ran to the science lab. There wasn't a class going on inside since the lab was currently being used to store all the science fair projects. Mount Vesuvius towered above the other projects, taking up a whole corner. The spider terrarium was back in its place by the window. Jaclyn put the potion into a beaker and heated it over a Bunsen burner. The liquid began to bubble. Jaclyn placed a glass thermometer inside. Paige and Fatima stared at her expectantly as she watched the red mercury rise.

"One hundred sixty-eight degrees exactly," said Jaclyn. "It's ready." She grabbed the beaker with her right hand, then held it up like she was giving a toast. "Goodbye forever, Jackie." As she brought the beaker to her lips, her left hand shot out and grabbed her right wrist. The nails were sharp. It was Jackie's hand.

"Not so fast!" said Jackie.

Paige and Fatima jumped back in terror. Jaclyn was half herself, half Jackie.

Her right pigtail was neatly combed, and her left was fraying out of the elastic. Her right eye was brown, while her left eye was green and scowling. Jaclyn's hand struggled against Jackie's, one trying to pull the beaker toward her mouth, the other trying to push it away.

"Come on, Jaclyn, stay strong!" Fatima shouted.

Jaclyn dug down deep and wrenched the beaker to her face, but Jackie bit her arm. Jaclyn cried out. Jackie wrestled with Jaclyn and flung her across the room—which also meant she flung herself across the room. By the time she pulled herself up, Jaclyn was gone. She was all Jackie.

Jackie whipped her head around to face Paige and Fatima. "Jackie's backie!"

"AAAGH!" Paige and Fatima screamed.

Jackie waved the potion above her head in

victory. Miraculously, it hadn't spilled out in the scuffle. "You think you can get rid of me?" she seethed. "Think again!"

She ran at full speed toward the science-lab door. Paige darted in front of her, blocking her way. Fatima tried to grab the potion from her, but she pushed her off, sending Fatima flying into the terrarium, knocking the lid off. The spiders scattered everywhere.

"Not again!" she cried.

Then, in a flash, Jackie grabbed the fire extinguisher off the wall. She clamped down on the nozzle. A cloud of white foam sprayed out, covering Paige from head to toe.

Paige wiped the foam from her eyes and Fatima pulled herself to her feet. But it was too late. The door to the science lab was open, and Jackie was gone.

Jackie tiptoed through the school, crouching down low whenever she passed a classroom window so she wouldn't be spotted.

All the while, she muttered to herself,

"Naughty, naughty Jaclyn tried to destroy me. Bad idea. Doesn't she know I'm trying to help her? That I'm her only real friend? I've got plans. Big plans!"

She scampered down the hallway of padlocked lockers and quietly pushed open the door to the cafeteria. Tanya was working in the back, thawing the frozen food for lunch. Jackie breathed in deeply through her nose. "Mm. Fish cakes." She drooled a little, then dropped to the floor and crawled under the tables toward the kitchen. She scooted around the counter and hid behind a stainless steel sink. She peered out and saw Tanya opening cans of green beans and dumping the contents into an aluminum serving tray. Next to her was a rack of trays filled with frozen french fries. Tanya emptied the last can of green beans, wiped her hands on her apron, and headed to the pantry.

Jackie knew that this was her chance. She snuck over to the rack and grabbed a tray. "Let's play a game," she whispered. She crammed the tray of fries into the oven, then turned the dial all the way up. "Hot potato!"

She ran back behind the sink and waited, hardly able to contain her glee.

By the time Tanya came back carrying a tub of ketchup, thin wisps of smoke were starting to seep out from the oven. "Huh?" She opened the oven and the smoke billowed out. "Oh my goodness!" Tanya said, clutching the edges of her paper hat. "Miss Carver's gonna kill me!" She threw on oven mitts, grabbed the tray, and tossed it in the sink. While she was busy flapping her apron up and down to clear the smoke, Jackie went to work.

She bolted across the kitchen to an enormous vat. She opened the lid. Inside was the day's batch of hot apple cider. "They think Jaclyn's bad. They don't even know what bad is." She laughed softly. Then she poured every last drop of the Perfection Potion into the cider.

CHAPTER SIXTEEN
Hyde and Seek

Jackie ran from the cafeteria through the empty hallways, delighted by what she had just done. The students sat quietly in their classrooms, oblivious to the fact that their beloved hot cider was about to turn them into their worst selves. Jackie snuck out the front door of the school and hopped onto Jaclyn's bike.

No! Jaclyn thought, though she didn't have a voice to say it. *I have to warn them!*

Jackie could hear Jaclyn's thoughts. "You can't warn them," she replied. "Won't you ever learn, Jaclyn? If you can't be perfect, *no one* will be perfect." Jackie pedaled down the street. "Don't worry, I'm in control now."

Jaclyn wanted to cry out for help, to slam on the bike brakes and run back to school. But she was locked in a fortress inside Jackie's body. And with every moment that passed, the walls got higher.

Jaclyn tried to shout, *Turn back!* But her shouts were merely nagging whispers in the back of Jackie's mind.

"Relax!" Jackie implored. "I'll take care of you." She skidded to a stop in front of Fog Island Hardware and ran inside.

The woman behind the counter eyed Jackie suspiciously. "Can I help you?" she asked.

"No. I'll help me!" Jackie said, grabbing a can of black spray paint from the shelf. She ran out of the store, cackling at the top of her lungs. She got back on the bike and pedaled away as fast as she could.

A bus drove by with an advertisement for the orchard on the side that said *Fog Island Apples: The Best in the World!* When the bus came to a stop, Jackie pulled up next to it and shook up the can of spray paint. She painted a line through the words *Fog Island Apples* and replaced them with *Jaclyn Hyde.*

The bus drove off. Jackie pumped her fist triumphantly. "Everyone will know the name Jaclyn Hyde!" She glanced around. "What's next?"

Jackie biked around the corner to a local art gallery. The bell on the door jingled as she walked in. She examined the paintings on the wall. There was a landscape of a dandelion field, more realistic than even Ryan Knowles could paint. A man walked in from the back, wearing a paint-splattered smock. He staggered backward at the sight of the small, scowling figure at the front of his shop, but he didn't want to be rude.

He cleared his throat. "Are you interested in that one? I painted it myself."

Jackie whipped her head around, her green eyes crackling with malice. "No, you didn't!" She took out the can and spray-painted *Jaclyn Hyde* over the artist's name.

"What are you doing?!" the gallery owner cried, charging toward her.

"I'm expressing myself!" Jackie shrieked. She ran out of the gallery, the owner at her heels, then jumped on the bike and sped away. He raced after her on foot, shouting at her furiously, but Jackie just laughed. She lost him as she reached the town square. An elderly man in a heavy coat fed breadcrumbs to a flock of pigeons, but otherwise it was empty. In the center of the square was a big brass statue of Penny Pogwilly. Jackie slowed down. She jumped off the bike, and it crashed to the ground. She crouched down in front of the statue and read the plaque: "In honor of Penny Pogwilly, the founder of Fog Island."

"Hmm." Jackie tapped her chin. "This needs just one small fix." She blacked out

Penny Pogwilly's name with the spray paint. In big sloppy letters on the concrete above it, she wrote *JACYLN HY—*

"Over there!" she heard.

Before she could finish, she saw the gallery owner and the woman from the hardware store standing next to a police officer. They were pointing right at her.

"Whoa—gotta boogie," said Jackie. She leaped on the bike and tore off down the block. She took a hard right into an alley and pumped the pedals as hard as she could.

"Can't get caught . . . can't get caught . . . ," she muttered to herself. "I know—how about a little Hyde and seek?"

She rode past the orchard and turned onto the street where Jaclyn lived. She heard the sound of a siren in the distance. She reached Jaclyn's house. She could see through the front window that Jaclyn's dad was at the kitchen table, working on his computer. Then she saw Jaclyn's mom driving up the street, heading home for lunch.

Jackie parked the bike around the side of the house where no one would see it, then ran to the back, searching frantically for a hiding place. She spotted the shed surrounded by weeds near the edge of the yard.

No! Jaclyn thought. *No one will ever find us in there.*

"Exactly!" said Jackie.

She ducked into the shed and closed the door behind her.

The shed was cold and drafty. The scent of mold lingered in the air. It was so packed with junk that there was barely enough room to move around inside. Jackie stepped over a half-empty bag of potting soil, careful to avoid a pair of rusty garden shears on the ground.

In the dim light, Jaclyn could barely see through Jackie's eyes. She was completely walled off in her fortress. She thought about Dr. Enfield's lab mice, and a chill ran through her.

Is this it? Jaclyn thought. *Am I trapped in here forever?*

"Don't be sad, Jaclyn," said Jackie. "It's better this way. You need me." Jackie ducked underneath a ladder and pushed aside a shovel that was leaning against a stack of old newspapers. She swatted away a cobweb that was hanging down from the ceiling. She had almost reached the back when she tripped on a cardboard box that was crammed in the corner.

She glanced down at the box. Written neatly in marker on the top were the words *DO NOT OPEN*.

Don't look in there! Jaclyn thought.

"Ooh! A secret! I like secrets!" said Jackie. She knelt down and opened the box. She picked up the first piece of paper she saw. It was the failed lava formula. Then, beneath it, a seventh grade algebra test with Jaclyn's name on it. At the top, circled in red marker, was the grade: C+.

Jackie's lip started to twitch. "What is this?"

She grabbed the next paper, Jaclyn's sixth grade essay on the American Revolution with a B- grade. Jackie's blood boiled as she dug through the box. There was a vote count announcement from the student council election when Jaclyn had come in third. A crumpled-up piece of piano music that Jaclyn had once tried to play but never mastered. A birthday card Jaclyn had made for her sister with the word *birthday* misspelled. Jackie saw all the evidence of Jaclyn's imperfections, a hidden history going all the way back to her kindergarten report card when she got a "Needs Improvement" in sharing.

Jackie trembled with rage. "What were you thinking?!" she snapped. "You fool! What kind of a hiding place is this? Right behind your house?" Then she saw the rest of the boxes. There was a whole stack of them, each box labeled *DO NOT OPEN*.

"What if someone found these boxes? How could you be so stupid? Oh, I know, because you're a C+ student. Because Jaclyn Hyde is the least perfect person to ever exist. This is exactly why you need me! This is exactly why I can't ever let you out again!" Jackie kicked the boxes, and the contents spilled out onto the floor.

Jaclyn was petrified. She felt like she was getting carved up by Miss Carver, except it was Jackie doing the ranting.

"I guess this is just one more thing I have to fix for you, Jaclyn!" Jackie stomped over to the dusty barbecue grill and lifted the lid. On the grate was a box of matches. She picked it up.

What are you doing? Jaclyn tried to scream.

"Destroying it all. You can thank me later," said Jackie. She took a match out of the box.

Jaclyn tried to fight against Jackie and somehow stop her from lighting the match. But it felt like the harder she fought, the weaker she became.

I hate you! Jaclyn shouted. *This is all your fault!*

Jackie struck the match.

In the light of the flame, Jaclyn saw all of the evidence of her failures scattered across the ground. One thing caught her eye. A pink, headless ceramic flamingo. Jaclyn hadn't seen it since she'd hidden it in the box in third grade.

But why had she hidden it in here in the first place? It wasn't her fault that the flamingo wasn't perfect.

And that's when she was hit with a vivid memory—

She was eight years old in the art studio with her class. She was rushing to finish painting her flamingo. She had told the whole class she could do it. But she was running out of time. In a moment of panic, she knocked the flamingo off the table. It fell to the ground, and its awkward bulbous head snapped off its dainty neck. She was so ashamed that without even thinking, she blamed the whole thing on Shane. He just happened to be sitting next to her at the time. It had been her fault all along.

Jaclyn realized that hiding her imperfections was what had caused all this in the first place. If she hadn't been so desperate to seem perfect, she wouldn't have made the potion. She wouldn't have created Jackie. This wasn't Jackie's fault. It was hers. Jaclyn had spent her whole life stuffing her mistakes into boxes and hoping no one would ever see. Now, she was done hiding.

The world has to know, Jaclyn thought.

"Know what?" said Jackie, moving toward the cardboard boxes, the match flickering in her hand.

That I'm not perfect! I've never been perfect! I'll never be perfect!

With that, Jaclyn felt a surge of strength. She stopped Jackie in her tracks.

Jackie's eyes bulged. She tried to take a step forward, but it was like her feet were glued to the floor.

I'm in charge now, thought Jaclyn.

"In your dreams!" Jackie hissed. She tried to throw the lit match at the boxes. But Jaclyn used all her strength to hold back Jackie's hand.

"Stop it! Stop it!" Jackie snarled, trying to wrest control of her own arm. But it was no use. The fortress walls around Jaclyn were crumbling. Jackie let out one final ear-splitting shriek, and then Jaclyn blew out the flame.

Jaclyn collapsed with relief. She looked at her spindly arms and ran her knobby hands through her frayed pigtails. Though she was still physically Jackie, Jaclyn was in control. She reached over and grabbed the nearest box. It was time to take it out of the shed, out into the open. As she picked it up, she heard a rustle behind the stack.

"Huh?"

She cleared away all the boxes. Deep in the corner was an old bag of wood chips. A hole had been gnawed in the plastic. Sitting next to the bag in a makeshift burrow was Charles.

"Charles! You came home!" Jaclyn cried, scooping him up into her arms. "I missed you so much! I'm sorry I lost you. Can you ever forgive me?"

Charles wiggled his nose. He nuzzled his soft fur into her neck.

A tear of joy ran down her cheek. "I'm pretty sure that's a yes."

CHAPTER SEVENTEEN
We're All Bad

Jaclyn's parents were very surprised when they answered the back door and found a green-eyed goblin girl on the step, holding a cardboard box and a rabbit. But when they realized that it was Jaclyn, Mom let her inside and Dad stopped screaming.

Jaclyn put the box and Charles down on the kitchen table and said, "I need help."

She explained everything. Enfield Manor.

The Perfection Potion. Losing Charles.

Dad interrupted, "But I saw Charles in his cage this morning!"

"That was a rolled-up ball of socks," Jaclyn admitted.

"I thought he looked a little lumpy," said Dad.

Jaclyn opened the box and showed her parents how she had spent years trying to hide her imperfections.

Mom sank down into a chair. There was a long silence. Jaclyn didn't know what was going to come next. Was she going to be in more trouble than she was in already?

"Jaclyn . . . ," Mom said, "I'm so sorry."

Jaclyn sat down next to her. "You are?"

"I didn't realize how much pressure we were putting on you. I just wanted you to live up to your potential. I've always known you could do great things. But growing up isn't about hiding your mistakes, it's about learning from them."

Dad joined them at the table. "I'm sorry, too,

Jaclyn. I know I didn't do a good job of showing it, but I'm not proud of you because you're perfect. I'm proud of you because you're you."

Jaclyn threw her arms around both her parents in a big hug. Her hands felt like sandpaper and she smelled like a rotten apple, but they didn't mind at all.

"Now how are we going to get you back to your old self?" said Mom.

"Not that we don't love your . . . new self," Dad said, eyeing her clawlike nails.

"Well," said Jaclyn, "if I could take one more dose of the—*oh no.*" Jaclyn looked at the clock. She had only now realized how much time had passed since she left school.

"What is it?" said Mom.

"I need you to drive me to school *now!*"

The car peeled into the school parking lot. Jaclyn leaped out, desperate to make it before the hot apple cider was served. Her parents followed close behind. She sprinted down the hall and pushed open the cafeteria doors. It was too late. The cafeteria tables were littered with empty crinkled paper cups. The entire school had already drunk the cider. The teachers and students chatted and nibbled at their lunches, totally oblivious to what was about to happen.

Paige and Fatima spotted Jaclyn in the doorway—but she still looked like Jackie. They jumped up from their seats and ran over to her.

"*You!*" Fatima sneered.

"Stay away!" Paige shouted, jabbing a plastic fork at her.

Jaclyn put her hands up. "I know I look like Jackie but it's me. I promise!"

"It's true," said Mom.

Dad added, "It's our Jaclyn, even though she looks absolutely terrifying. No offense, sweetie."

Jaclyn looked anxiously at Paige and Fatima. "You didn't drink the cider, did you?"

"No, we never drink the cider," said Fatima. Then her eyes grew wide. "Why?"

Before Jaclyn could explain, the sound of a

thousand joints cracking filled the room. Everyone around them began to transform. Their faces contorted into surly grimaces. Their nails sharpened and their eyes glowed green.

"What's happening?" Paige squeaked.

As Fatima saw her teachers and classmates morph into their fiendish alter egos, she figured it out. "Jackie put the Perfection Potion in the cider, didn't she?"

Jaclyn gulped. "Uh-huh. And it looks like they got a much stronger dose than I did."

The friendly chatter from moments before was replaced with shouts and snarls. Everyone's worst impulses were unleashed. Their deepest desires were pushed to the surface. And they would stop at nothing to get what they wanted.

Zeke was now twice his normal size, his muscles bulging from his too-tight turtleneck like he was the Hulk. He flipped an entire cafeteria table over with a thunderous crash and bellowed, "Who's the pip-squeak now?!"

Marina leaped on top of a table and started

tap-dancing, kicking over milk cartons and stomping on baskets of french fries. She sang at the top of her lungs, but her once-melodic voice had transformed into a nightmarish screech.

Ryan Knowles darted around, collecting every ketchup and mustard bottle he could find. Then he turned the room into a giant canvas, squirting sauces across the wall in broad strokes and splattering anyone who got in his way. "Bow down to my masterpiece," he shouted.

Jaclyn put face in her hands. "This is even worse than I thought."

"Look!" said Paige, pointing across the room. There was one last cup of cider on the edge of the counter by the cash register.

"It must be your cider, Jaclyn," said Fatima. "Paige gave hers to Marina. And I gave mine to Mr. Collins."

Mr. Collins, wearing the head of the moose costume, plowed into a cluster of teachers with his antlers.

"I wish I hadn't."

"Come on, let's get it," said Jaclyn.

The girls pushed their way through the fray. They were about to reach the counter when Tanya leaped out from the kitchen, brandishing a metal pan. A vein bulged above her eye. "Who's going to serve *me* lunch?!" she screamed, smashing the pan onto the tub of green beans. She made her way down the counter, flipping over trays of food. She swung the pan wildly, shattering the sneeze guard, and nearly crashed into the cup of cider, but Jaclyn got there just in time. She grabbed the cup and ducked underneath a table. Paige and Fatima crouched down next to her.

"Drink it!" said Paige.

Jaclyn looked down at the cider. This was her chance to go back to her old self for good. But she couldn't do it.

"Come on!" said Fatima. "Get rid of Jackie once and for all!"

"But then what will happen to everyone else?" said Jaclyn. "This is my fault. I have to fix it."

"How?" said Fatima. "There's only one cup left."

Jaclyn didn't know what to say.

"Wait—" said Paige. "Where are your mom and dad?"

Jaclyn looked around the cafeteria and gasped. "Mr. Collins got them!"

Mr. Collins was using an extension cord to tie Jaclyn's parents down to the bench in front of the table where Marina was performing. Once they were secured to the seat, Mr. Collins hopped up onto the table, too. Marina and Mr. Collins broke into a duet that sounded like shards of glass going through a meat grinder. Around them, everyone was getting more and more out of control.

Jaclyn could barely hear herself think. But she had to think of something. She put her hands on her head and looked at the chaos, an expression of utter terror on her face. "What a disaster!"

"Wow," said Fatima. "You look exactly like one of the figurines I painted at the base of Mount Vesuvius."

Jaclyn gasped. "That's it! The volcano!"

Paige cocked her head. "Huh?"

"We can mix this last cup of cider in with the lava, set off the eruption, and it'll splatter all over everyone in the cafeteria!"

Fatima's jaw dropped. "You're a genius. We've got to get to the science lab."

"Fast," Paige added. "Or else somebody's going to get hurt. Probably Mr. Hanh."

Mr. Hanh had stolen a box of brownies from the kitchen. He was shoveling them into his mouth while Tanya chased him around, trying to hit him in the head with the pan.

As the girls crawled out from under the table, the doors to the cafeteria burst open with such force, they nearly broke off their hinges. Miss Carver stood in the doorway. It looked like her head was going to explode. "What is going on here?!"

Shane climbed onto a chair and grinned. His teeth had warped and sharpened so that the wires of his braces snapped. "We're bad," he declared. "We're all bad!" He picked up a handful of french fries and chucked them at her head.

Miss Carver chased after Shane, but she was sidetracked when she saw Todd and Davis rampaging around, ripping open every backpack in sight and stealing whatever lunch money they found inside.

"I'm going to buy an ostrich!" Todd shouted.

"I'm going to buy a whole chicken farm!" Davis screeched.

Miss Carver banged on the table and bellowed, "Stop it! Stop it this instant!" but no one paid any attention. She stomped around, berating every student in sight. "I've said it from day one! You're all bad apples! This is *my* school! Do you know how this makes me look? I've never been so humiliated in my life!" Then she saw the back wall. It was coated from floor to ceiling in ketchup and mustard. Ryan stood proudly in front of it, admiring his work. Miss Carver shrieked at the top of her lungs.

"Now's our chance," said Jaclyn.

The girls snuck out of the cafeteria.

CHAPTER EIGHTEEN
An Onion Sandwich

As Jaclyn, Paige, and Fatima ran through the empty halls, they could hear the muffled chaos coming from the cafeteria. They reached the science lab and found their volcano against the back wall. Jaclyn opened the cabinet with the chemistry supplies and got to work. She had never moved so fast in her life. Her hands flew between beakers and test tubes, concocting her proprietary lava formula. When she'd first made it, she'd thought it was a total failure, but not anymore. A massive explosion was exactly what she needed.

"I sure hope I can repeat my mistake."

"You can do it, Jaclyn," Paige grunted as she and Fatima lifted the volcano onto a supply cart.

Fatima's knees almost buckled. "Why is this thing so heavy? I thought it was papier-mâché."

"Mostly . . . ," said Jaclyn. "But I *may* have added some volcanic rocks to the base."

Fatima and Paige stared at her.

"What? I wanted to make it realistic!"

Jaclyn finished making the lava. She combined it with the cup of apple cider in a beaker, then plugged it closed. Then she poured a tablespoon of baking soda into the volcano and said, "Let's go."

Together, they rolled the volcano toward the cafeteria. As they got closer, they could hear the wild shouts coming from inside, even louder than before. Paige grabbed the door handles and pulled. But the doors wouldn't budge.

Frantically, she tried again, but still nothing. "It's locked!" she said.

"Oh no . . ." Jaclyn pushed her face up against the crack between the double doors. She peered down and saw a padlock keeping them shut from the inside.

Miss Carver was standing at the center of the pandemonium. "You see what you've made me do?" she yelled. "You animals don't deserve to be in a school, you deserve to be in a zoo! That's exactly why I've locked you in here! Until you stop this madness, I'm not unlocking that door for anything!"

Jaclyn banged on the doors. "Miss Carver, let us in!"

But no one inside could hear her.

They kept banging until a voice from down the hall got their attention. "There you are!" Shane was walking toward them with a devilish smile. The frayed wires of his braces looked like the whiskers of an unhinged cat. He was holding a can of Caffeine-Free Diet Blue in his hand.

"Trying to show off your science fair project?" He slipped into his Jaclyn impression. "I'm Jaclyn Hyde. I'm going to win the science fair." He shook up the can. "I don't think so."

He hurled the soda straight at the volcano.

"Look out!" said Paige.

The girls leaped to the side. The can hit the top of Mount Vesuvius, chipping off the edge, then exploded against the wall.

"What are you doing? You almost broke it," Jaclyn cried.

"Next time it won't be *almost*." He flung open the door to the custodian's closet. He pulled out a gallon jug of hand soap and chucked it at the volcano. Paige smacked it out of the air, and it hit the floor, spilling everywhere.

Shane wasn't deterred. He reached back into the closet and this time, he pulled out a heavy snow shovel. He moved toward the volcano, swinging the shovel like baseball bat.

"Don't even think about it, you sack of worm eggs," said Fatima.

Fatima and Jaclyn grabbed the cart and rolled the volcano backward as quickly as they could. Paige ran at Shane, but she slipped in the liquid soap and fell.

Shane laughed hysterically.

Fatima ran over to help Paige up, and Shane ran past them, swinging the shovel wildly.

Jaclyn stood in front of the volcano and held out her arms. "Shane, stop!"

"Shane's not here right now," he spat, his eyes glowing green.

"I know he's in there somewhere, and I need to say something to him—something I should have said a long, long time ago."

He raised the shovel high above his head and was just about to bring it down to crush the volcano when Jaclyn said, "Shane, I'm sorry!"

He stopped midswing. "Huh?"

"You were right. You've been right ever since third grade. You didn't break the flamingo. I did. I just didn't want to admit it. I had told the whole class that I was going to make this perfect flamingo and then I ruined it. I was so desperate to believe I hadn't made a mistake that I convinced myself it was your fault."

Shane's glared at her. "Everyone thought I was a liar. A bad kid. They still do."

"I know. I didn't realize what I had done to you. Sure, it's hard when people expect you to be perfect all the time, but it's a thousand times harder when they don't believe in you at all. I didn't know that until today."

Shane's eyes darted back and forth. It looked like his brain was short-circuiting. Then he dropped the shovel and it clattered to the ground.

Fatima gingerly picked it up. "I'm just going to hold on to this."

Shane looked down at his knobbly hands and ran his tongue along his broken braces. It was like he was noticing that he was wearing a Halloween costume and he didn't remember putting it on.

"What happened to me? What happened to you? What happened to everybody?"

"I'll explain later. The important thing is I can fix it if I can get through these doors. But Miss Carver said she won't unlock them for anything."

A smile slowly crept across Shane's face. "Leave that to me." He turned to Paige. "Sorry about the soap."

Paige shrugged. "It's okay. These pants needed to be washed anyway."

He took off down the hall.

"Hey, Shane," Jaclyn called after him.

He looked back. "What?"

"We believe in you."

He nodded and ran around the corner.

The girls looked at each other.

"What do you think he's going to do?" said Fatima.

"I have no idea," said Jaclyn.

Moments later, the PA system crackled to life, and Shane's voice came blaring through. "Good afternoon, students. Or should I say— bad afternoon! I'm coming to you live from the most forbidden place in the entire school. That's right. I'm in Miss Carver's office."

Jaclyn, Paige, and Fatima crowded together at the cafeteria doors and peeked through them. They could see Miss Carver looking up at the PA speaker, her expression a perfect storm of confusion and fury.

Shane continued, "Let's take a look around, shall we? Ooh, Miss Carver's lunch bag. I wonder what's in here. An onion sandwich? Wow. That is so gross and not surprising at all."

Miss Carver threw a chair at the speaker. It hit the wall and clattered to the ground.

"Oh, look!" said Shane. "There's a dartboard with all our pictures on it. Maybe Fatima could write an article about it for the school paper. I'm sure our parents would *love* to know about that."

Everyone in the cafeteria was listening to Shane's every word.

Over the PA system was the sound of a drawer opening. "What's in here? Our disciplinary records? Well, these are going straight in the shredder. And what's this? The control panel to the electronic sign in front of the school? I can write any message I want?"

By now, Miss Carver was practically foaming at the mouth.

"How about . . . 'My name is Miss Carver and I'm the worst principal in the history of the world. And I smell like a corpse.'"

Miss Carver couldn't take it anymore. "I'll get you, you rotten little toad!" She ran to the door and put the key in the lock.

"Look out!" said Jaclyn.

Jaclyn, Paige, and Fatima rolled the volcano behind the corner and ducked out of sight just as Miss Carver burst out of the doors. In a blind rage, she tore off toward her office.

The coast was clear.

CHAPTER NINETEEN
It's Been a Long Time

Jaclyn, Fatima, and Paige pushed the volcano into the cafeteria. The whole place was in shambles. There was food everywhere. Teachers were yelling and students were fighting, destroying everything around them in the process.

"Where should we put this thing?" said Jaclyn. "We need the lava to hit *everybody*."

Fatima pointed to the table in the center of the room. "How about there?"

It was the only table left upright—Zeke had flipped the rest. It was also the stage for Marina and Mr. Collins's two-person show. They were still tap-dancing on the table. Marina was singing in her screechiest voice, and Mr. Collins was dancing next to her in his moose costume.

Jaclyn's parents were still tied up on the bench in front of them, forced to be their audience. However, now they were also being forced to hold heat lamps from the cafeteria kitchen so Marina and Mr. Collins could each have a spotlight. Sweat dripped down Dad's forehead.

"This is the worst show I have ever seen," he said.

"Make it stop," Mom cringed.

"This is a five-act extravaganza, and we're only on the first scene," Marina snarled at them.

"We've got to help them," said Jaclyn.

They pushed the cart through the crowd as quickly as they could, but it wasn't easy. Their deranged classmates were darting out in front of them from every direction, and they had to steer around benches and tables that were strewn everywhere. The wheels skidded on some spilled milk and the whole thing almost tipped over. Paige used all her strength to keep the volcano upright.

They were getting close to the center of the cafeteria when Todd leaped on Jaclyn's back like a toddler who'd just eaten a bag of sugar for lunch.

Davis grabbed her arm. "Give me all your money!"

"I don't have any money!" said Jaclyn, trying to buck Todd off her back while wriggling her arm free from Davis.

"Hey, maybe we can sell that volcano!" said Todd.

Paige stepped in front of the cart and held out her arms to keep the sixth graders away from the volcano.

Fatima ran over to Ryan Knowles. His ketch-up-and-mustard painting now covered all four walls and much of the floor, but he showed no sign of stopping. Fatima snatched the ketchup and mustard bottles out of his hands and ran back toward Jaclyn.

"I'm not done yet!" Ryan called after her.

"Paige, catch," Fatima said, tossing her the mustard bottle.

In perfect unison, Fatima squirted the ketchup into Todd's face while Paige squirted the mustard into Davis's. Todd fell off Jaclyn's back and onto the floor. Davis turned around and ran straight into a wall.

Now was their chance. The girls zigzagged the rest of the way until they finally reached the table in the center of the room.

"Jaclyn, you're back," Mom said with relief.

"Middle school is so much worse than I remember," Dad blubbered.

Jaclyn began untying her parents. Fatima unplugged the heat lamps.

Marina froze in the middle of her dance. "How dare you turn off my spotlight," she hissed.

Paige jumped up and popped the moose head off Mr. Collins. "Hey, Zeke. Catch," she said, hurtling the head across the room. Zeke caught it and grinned. Then he crushed it between his hands.

"No!" Mr. Collins cried. He hopped off the table and ran toward Zeke.

"Mr. Collins, wait!" Marina wailed, running after him. "The show must go on!" With the table now empty, Paige and Fatima hoisted the volcano on top of it. Jaclyn untied the last of the extension cord that was binding her parents to the bench. Mom and Dad leaped to their feet.

"You guys have to get out of here before the volcano erupts," said Jaclyn. She turned to Paige and Fatima. "And you, too. The last thing I need is for my best friends to turn into monsters."

Fatima and Paige shot each other a look.

"Yeah," said Fatima dryly. "I wonder what *that* would be like."

Paige and Fatima led Jaclyn's parents toward the door, but before they could get out, Miss Carver burst in, pulling Shane by his ear.

"Get in here with the rest of the animals," she screamed. Then she locked the doors behind her again.

"Quick—over here," said Fatima. She and Paige pulled Jaclyn's parents into the kitchen. They all crouched behind the counter, holding cafeteria trays above their heads for extra protection.

Miss Carver's eyes narrowed at Jaclyn, who was standing on the table next to the volcano.

"What are you doing?" she barked.

"Don't worry, Miss Carver. I'm going to fix everything."

She arched an eyebrow. "What do you mean?"

"Everyone in here got poisoned with Perfection Potion, and it's all my fault." She held up the beaker full of lava and cider. "This will change everyone back to normal."

"No, don't do that!" Miss Carver snapped.

Jaclyn looked at her with utter confusion. "Why not?"

"Because—" Miss Carver's expression

shifted. Her scowl vanished, and she spoke gently. "Because you're perfect just the way you are, Jaclyn." She took a step closer. "Why don't you put down that beaker and forget about it."

Jaclyn couldn't believe what she was hearing. "Why would I do that?"

Miss Carver forced a cloying smile. "I'll make you the star of every play."

"You chained the doors of the theater shut."

Miss Carver held up her key ring. "I'll unchain them. And I'll make you star artist of the week. Or better yet, star artist for life! And guess what? You've won the science fair."

"But it hasn't even started . . ."

"Who cares? Look at that magnificent volcano—I can tell you deserve first prize." A bead of sweat ran down her forehead. "I've got the ribbon in my office. Just put down the beaker."

Jaclyn looked at the mixture in her hand. Then she looked back at Miss Carver.

"Come on, Jaclyn. I'm offering you everything you ever wanted."

Jaclyn shook her head. "I don't want it anymore." She uncorked the beaker. "Miss Carver, stand back."

Miss Carver's nostrils flared. She charged at Jaclyn like a bull all the way across the cafeteria, releasing a thunderous shout of anger. She reached up and grabbed Jaclyn's wrist, her nails digging into her flesh. "GIVE ME THAT PERFECTION POTION."

Out of nowhere, Paige came flying through the air and crashed into Miss Carver, tackling her to the ground and knocking the wind out of her.

"You really should let me be on the football team," said Paige.

"Now!" Fatima shouted to Jaclyn from behind the counter.

Jaclyn poured the mixture into the volcano, and it began to bubble.

Paige rolled under the table and grabbed

Miss Carver by her legs, pulling her to safety as Mount Vesuvius exploded with spectacular inaccuracy. Cider and lava rained down on the cafeteria, splattering onto every student and teacher in the room. Now *everyone* resembled the painted figurines at the base of the volcano as they ran in all different directions.

Then, all at once, everyone stopped in their tracks. A sound rippled through the room like a massive exhale as the monstrous alter egos dissolved. Limbs untwisted. Bodies returned to their normal sizes. The toxic green in everyone's eyes faded away.

Jaclyn looked down at her hands. They were soft and smooth, her nails no longer sharp. She felt her pigtails, which were neatly combed without a single frayed hair.

Fatima, Mom, and Dad crawled out from behind the counter. Paige popped up from under the table. When they saw Jaclyn, they all beamed.

"Welcome back," said Fatima.

Suddenly, they heard a howling scream. Miss

Carver was writhing on the floor, a drop of lava dripping down her cheek.

"Oh no," said Jaclyn.

"I tried to pull her out of the way," said Paige.

Miss Carver clutched her chest and her eyes went wide. "Jaclyn! What have you done?" She writhed around, twisting in agony.

Fatima went pale. "Miss Carver is going to turn even more evil."

"How is that possible?" Paige said, horrified.

But then, Miss Carver's hunched back straightened. Her long hair broke free from the tight braid and sprang into bright red curls. Her permanent scowl melted into a warm smile.

As she stood up, Jaclyn instantly recognized her. "Greta Goodman?"

The woman walked over, took Jaclyn's hands, and looked her right in the eye. "It's been a long time since anyone has called me that."

CHAPTER TWENTY
The Happiest Moment

Jaclyn walked into the crowded lobby of the Fog Island Playhouse. It was December now, and the fog outside was crystalizing into a thin layer of frost.

"There you are," said Fatima. "I was worried you were going to be late."

Jaclyn checked her watch. "I would never be late to the professional premiere of *Fog Island: The Musical.*"

Fatima smiled. "Well, it wouldn't be happening without you."

Jaclyn had felt so terrible about ruining the school's production that she had taken it upon herself to submit the script to the community theater. They had accepted it right away.

Henry and Greta Goodman walked through the theater's front door arm in arm. Greta was wearing big snowflake-shaped earrings that sparkled against her red curls. Henry had on a fresh pair of overalls.

"There's our star writer!" Greta said, handing Fatima a bouquet of purple flowers.

"Technically, I'm only the cowriter. But I'll take all the flowers anyway," Fatima said.

Greta gestured around the lobby. "Isn't this amazing? Just one more reason to be proud of my students."

"They really are a remarkable bunch," said Henry, looking at Jaclyn with a twinkle in his eye.

After the lava explosion had turned her back to normal, Greta had run all the way to

Enfield Manor to find her estranged husband, Henry. She'd told him that years earlier, she had discovered that Dr. Enfield was working on a Perfection Potion. Even though she knew she was a good principal, she had always thought she could be better. She thought she could be perfect. Secretly, she took some of the Perfection Potion for herself. She knew right away that she'd made a mistake, but she couldn't figure out a way to reverse it. It didn't take long for Miss Carver to take over her body entirely. Without Jaclyn, she would have stayed that way forever. The letter Henry had found saying Greta was leaving him was really written by Miss Carver. Greta had never wanted to leave Henry. When she returned and explained it all, it was the happiest moment of Henry's life.

"Oh good—I made it! Practice went long," said Paige, running into the theater. She was wearing a big puffy coat over a mud-caked football uniform. She had joined the team as a linebacker just in time for playoffs.

"You ready for the big game this weekend?" Greta asked.

Paige smiled wide. "We're going to crush 'em, Mrs. G."

Shane's voice cut through the crowd. "Five minutes until curtain!" He flickered the lobby lights on and off.

Jaclyn hurried over to him. "Hey, Shane. Have a great show. It's so cool that you're the assistant stage manager."

"Thanks. They have a much bigger budget than at school. I'm in charge of six different fog machines!"

"I can't wait to see it," said Jaclyn.

"You won't be able to see much." He grinned. "It's going to get *really* foggy in there."

Jaclyn laughed. "Will you tell Marina 'break a leg' for me? She must be so excited to be in her first professional production."

"I'll tell her as soon as I see her. I think she's still getting into her tree costume." He looked at his clipboard. "I've got to run. I still have some props to set." He hurried backstage.

Jaclyn turned around and saw Mr. Hanh at the concession stand. Todd and Davis were behind the counter.

"These are the best chocolate chip cookies I've ever eaten!" Mr Hanh exclaimed.

"We couldn't have done it without Jaclyn," said Todd. "She gave us the recipe for Grandma Hyde's Chocolate Delights."

"We're raising money to start a whale-watching club," said Davis.

"I hope you're not planning to buy an actual whale," Jaclyn joked.

"We hadn't thought of that," said Todd.

Davis tapped his chin. "How many cookies do you think we'd have to sell?"

Fatima and Paige walked over and each put an arm around Jaclyn.

"Come on, let's get some good seats," said Paige.

"Excuse me," said Fatima. "I'm the coplaywright. It's all taken care of."

The girls went into the theater and made their way toward the stage. They waved to their parents, who were all sitting together, laughing and talking. Then they took their reserved seats in the front row next to Mr. Collins.

"This is so thrilling!" he exclaimed. "Everyone is going to love act three."

"Act three?" asked Jaclyn.

"I added a whole section about Enfield Manor," said Fatima. "I couldn't let all that valuable research go to waste. Plus, we needed to put in the moose dream sequence."

Jaclyn and Paige looked at her in surprise.

She leaned over to them and whispered, "It means a lot to Mr. Collins—and it honestly turned out pretty great."

Mr. Collins clapped his hands. "I've never been more excited for anything in my life!"

Jaclyn spotted Greta and Henry across the aisle. "I forgot to say thank you for the lab equipment."

After Greta and Henry had reunited, they'd decided to move from the small cottage on Dr.

Enfield's estate into the manor. They cleared out all the cobwebs and dusty furniture and gave all the lab equipment to Jaclyn.

"Of course," said Greta. She tapped her forehead. "A powerful young mind needs some powerful lab equipment."

"I'm already putting it to good use. I've made some major improvements to the lava formula."

"Jaclyn!" Paige exclaimed. "You already won the blue ribbon."

Mrs. Goodman had awarded the volcano project first place in the science fair. Even though it technically hadn't erupted *during* the science fair, it was by far the most life-changing science project in the history of Fog Island Middle School.

Fatima shook her head. "You *still* want to make it more realistic?"

"Nope," said Jaclyn. "I want to make an even bigger explosion!"

Jaclyn had found that once she wasn't worried about being perfect anymore, she had a lot more energy to focus on what she really cared about. She was most happy experimenting with her chemistry set and dreaming up new ideas. Once she was happy with the lava formula, she planned to move onto her next invention: edible wood chips for Charles.

As the lights dimmed and the musicians played the opening notes of "This Land Is Fog Land," Jaclyn smiled at her two best friends. Maybe she wasn't perfect, but this moment certainly was.

Also by
ANNABETH BONDOR-STONE
and
CONNOR WHITE!

SHIVERS!